ZIG
AND
WIKKI

IN

SOMETHING ATE
MY HOMEWORK

NADJA SPIEGELMAN & TRADE LOEFFLER

ZIG AND WIKKI

IN

SOMETHING ATE MY HOMEWORK

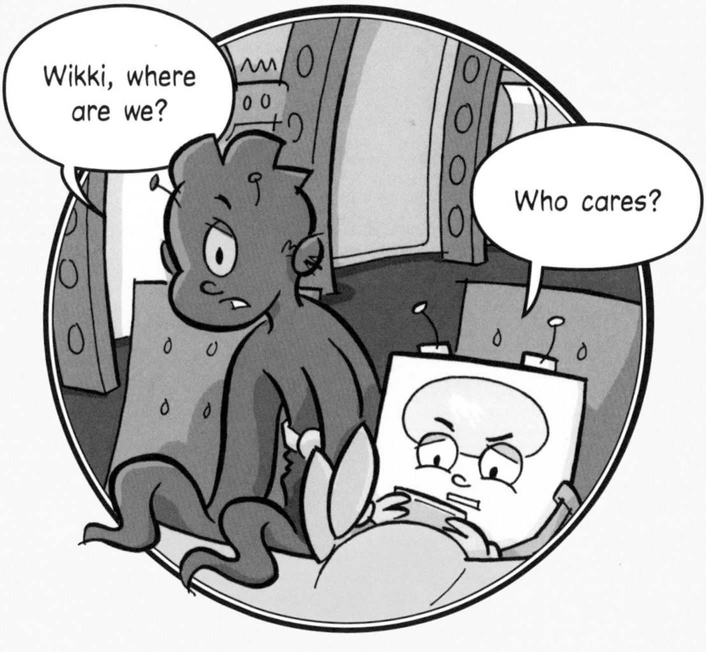
Wikki, where are we?
Who cares?

A TOON BOOK BY

NADJA SPIEGELMAN & TRADE LOEFFLER

TOON BOOKS, A DIVISION OF RAW JUNIOR, LLC, NEW YORK

For my mother

–Nadja

For Mohammad Riza

–Trade

Editorial Director: FRANÇOISE MOULY
Advisor: ART SPIEGELMAN

Book Design: FRANÇOISE MOULY & JONATHAN BENNETT

Guest Editor: GEOFFREY HAYES
Guest Nature Researcher: JUDY FUNK

A TOON BOOK

Library of Congress Cataloging-in-Publication Data
Spiegelman, Nadja.
Zig and Wikki in something ate my homework / a toon book by Nadja Spiegelman & Trade Loeffler.
p. cm.
Summary: Zig and Wikki arrive on earth to seach for a pet for Zig's class assignment.
ISBN 978-1-935179-02-3
1. Graphic novels. [1. Graphic novels. 2. Pets–Fiction. 3. Science fiction.] I. Loeffler, Trade, ill. II. Title.
PZ7.7.S65Zi 2010
[Fic]–dc22

2009028017
ISBN 13: 978-1-935179-02-3 ISBN 10: 1-935179-02-0
10 9 8 7 6 5 4 3 2 1

www.TOON-BOOKS.com

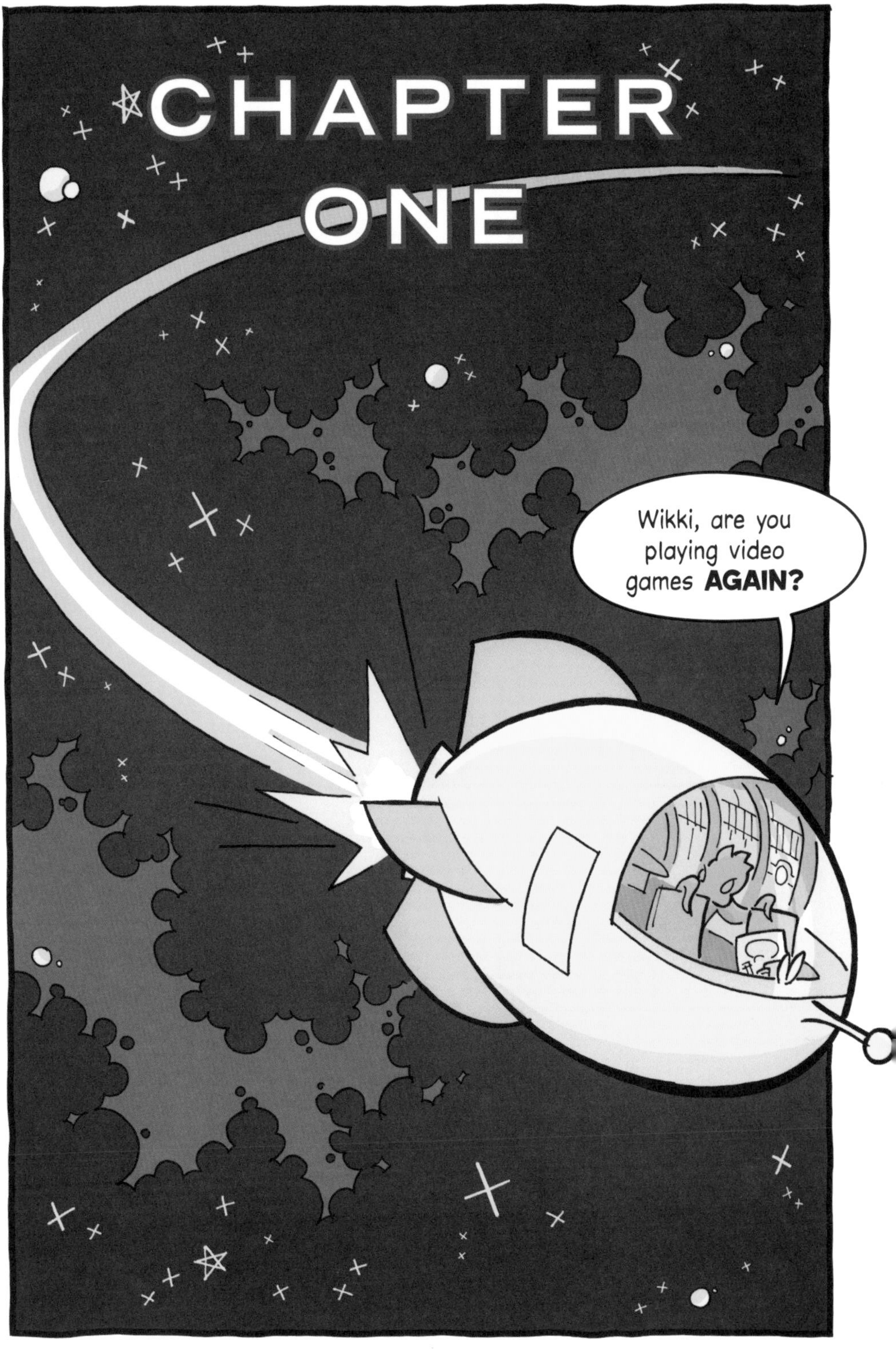
CHAPTER ONE
Wikki, are you playing video games **AGAIN?**

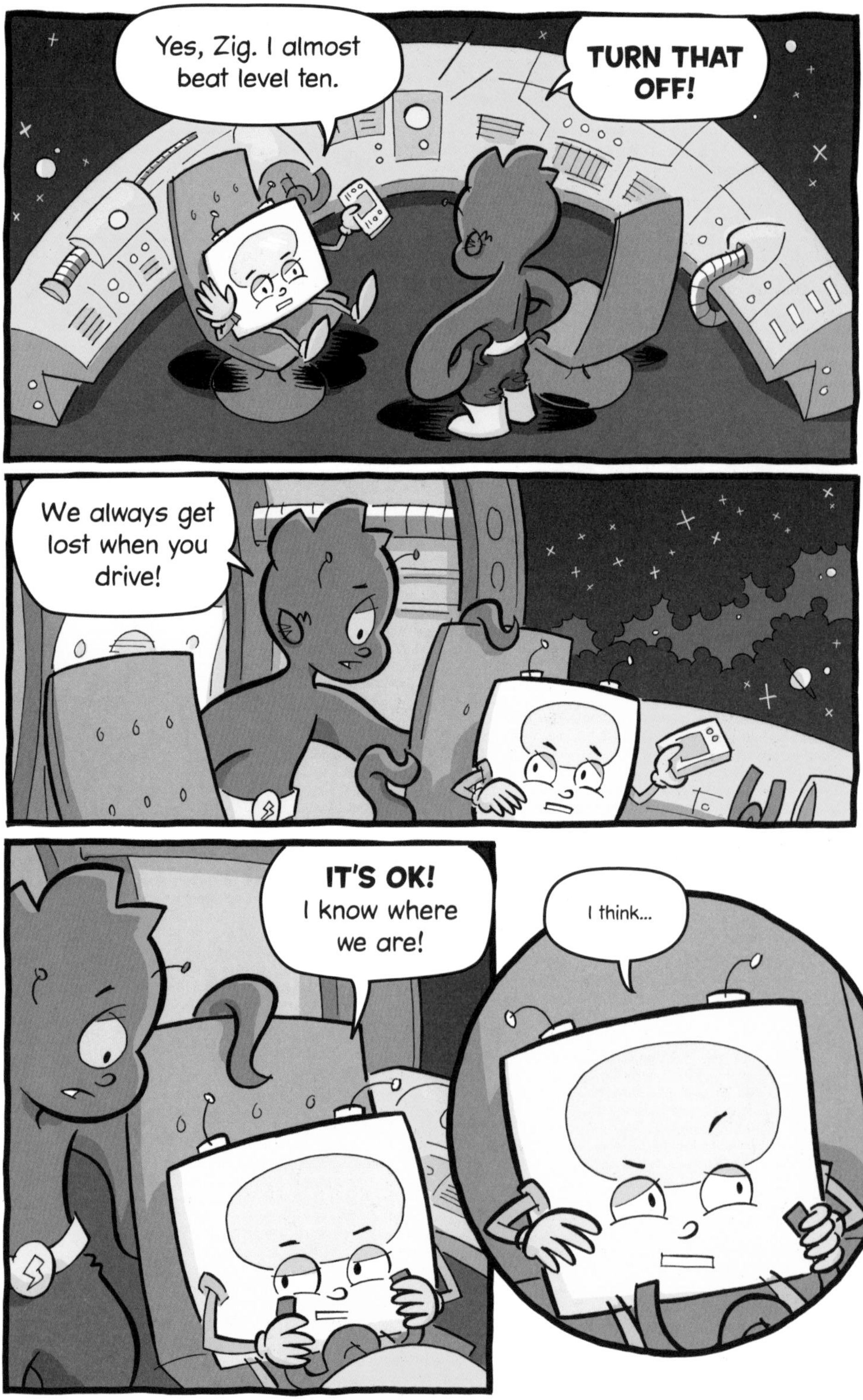
Yes, Zig. I almost beat level ten.
TURN THAT OFF!
We always get lost when you drive!
IT'S OK! I know where we are!
I think...

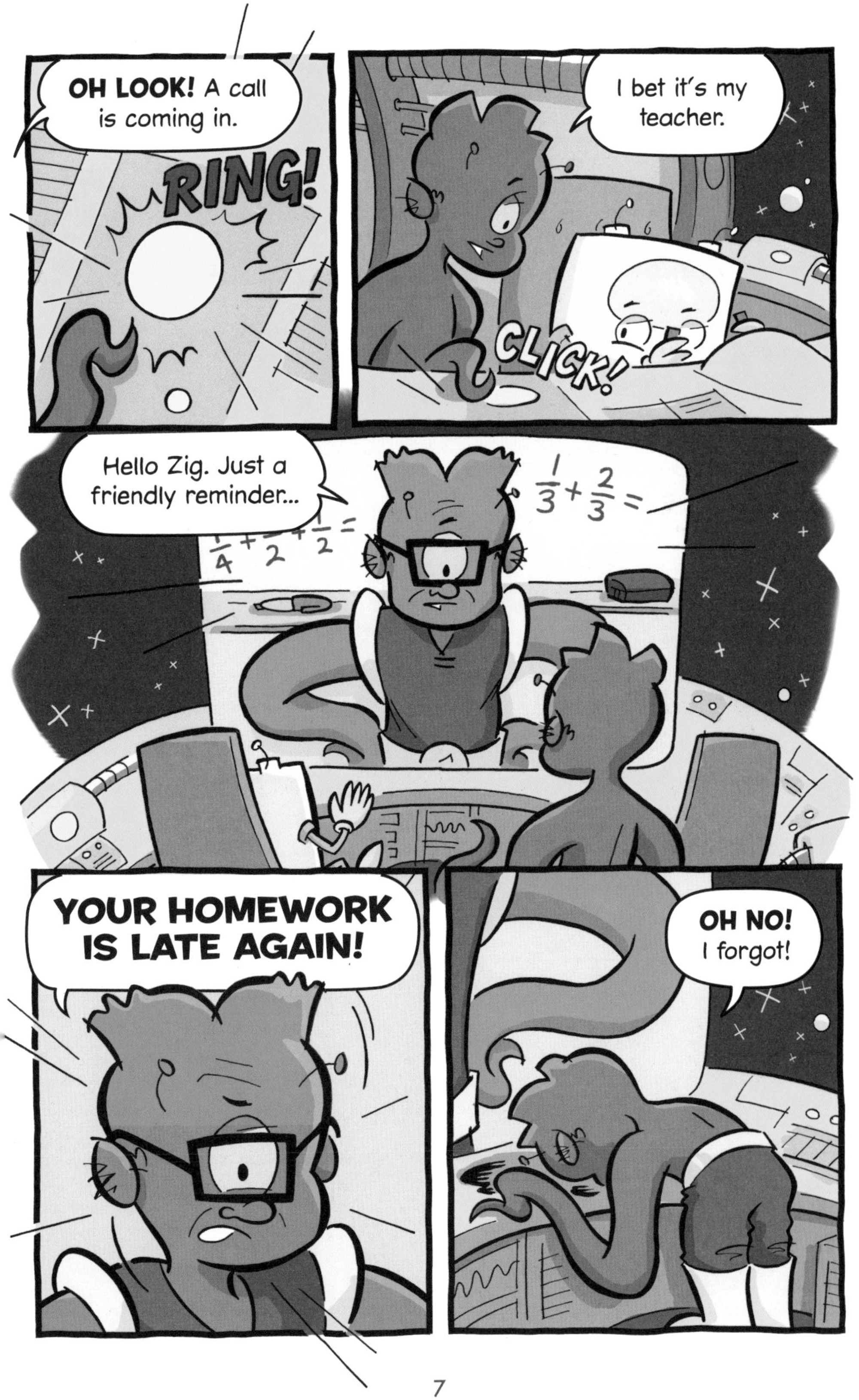
OH LOOK! A call is coming in.
RING!
I bet it's my teacher.
CLICK!
Hello Zig. Just a friendly reminder...
$\frac{1}{4} + \frac{1}{2} + \frac{1}{2} =$
$\frac{1}{3} + \frac{2}{3} =$
YOUR HOMEWORK IS LATE AGAIN!
OH NO! I forgot!

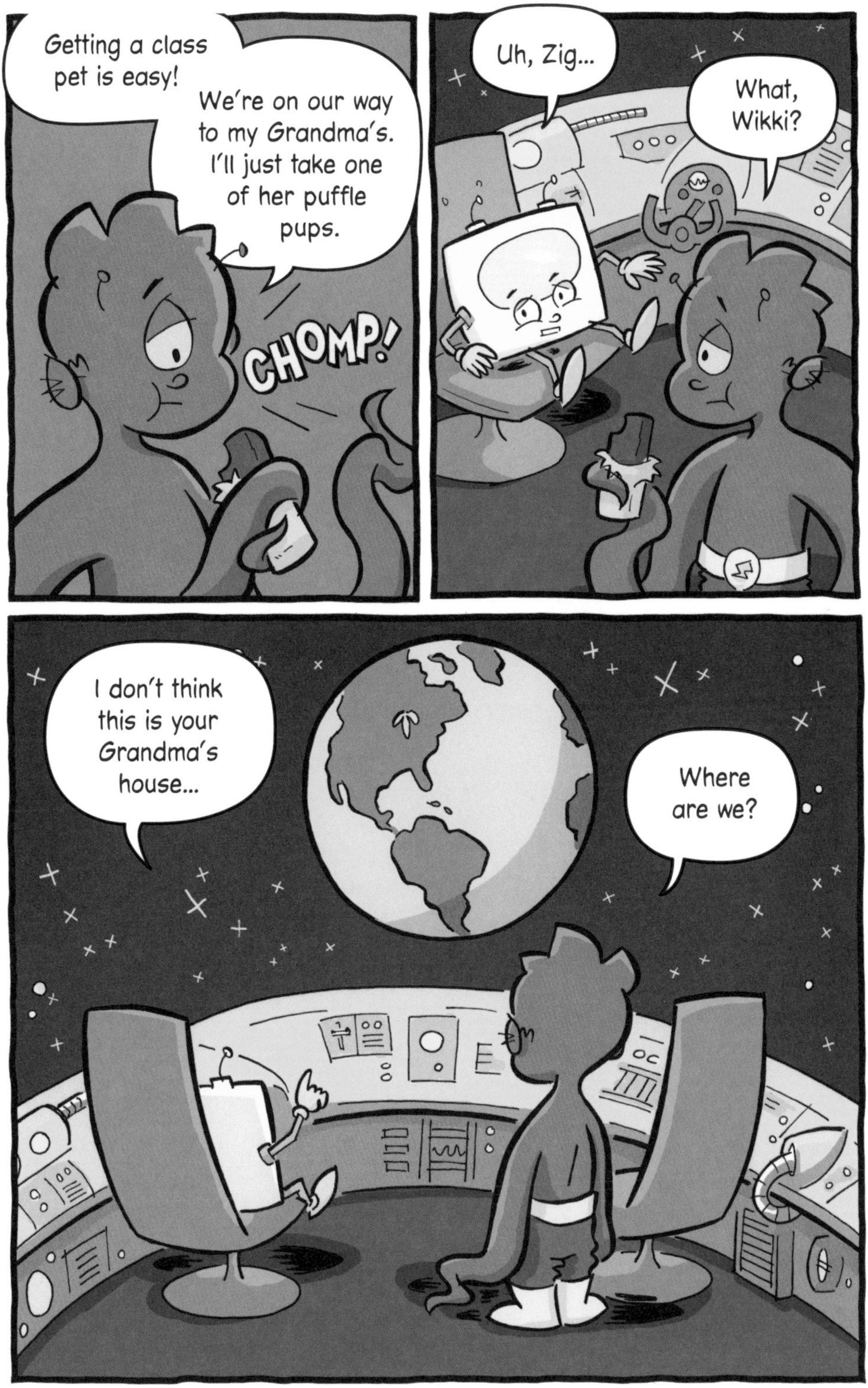
Getting a class pet is easy!
We're on our way to my Grandma's. I'll just take one of her puffle pups.
CHOMP!
Uh, Zig...
What, Wikki?
I don't think this is your Grandma's house...
Where are we?

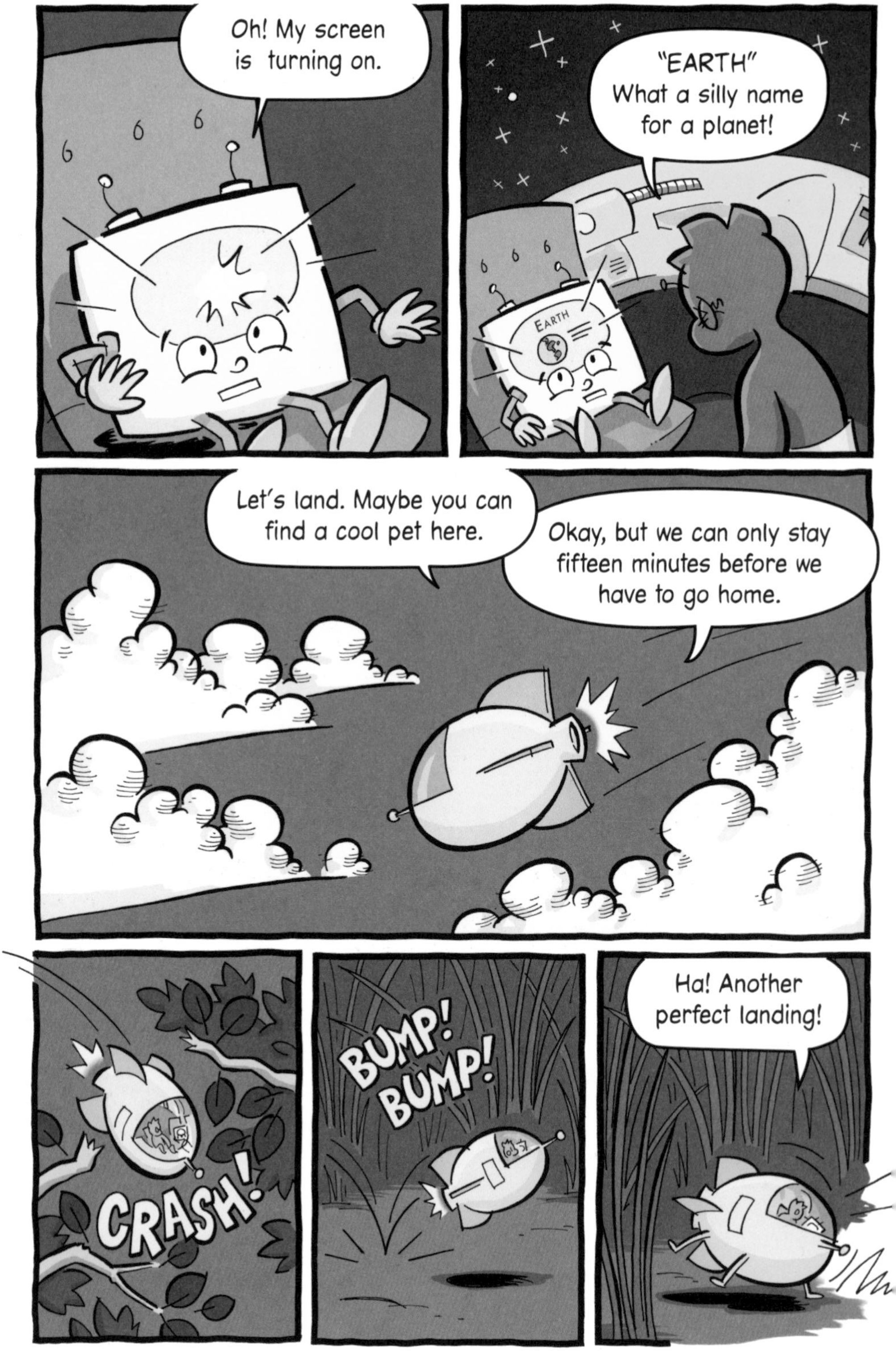
Oh! My screen is turning on.
"EARTH" What a silly name for a planet!
EARTH
Let's land. Maybe you can find a cool pet here.
Okay, but we can only stay fifteen minutes before we have to go home.
CRASH!
BUMP! BUMP!
Ha! Another perfect landing!

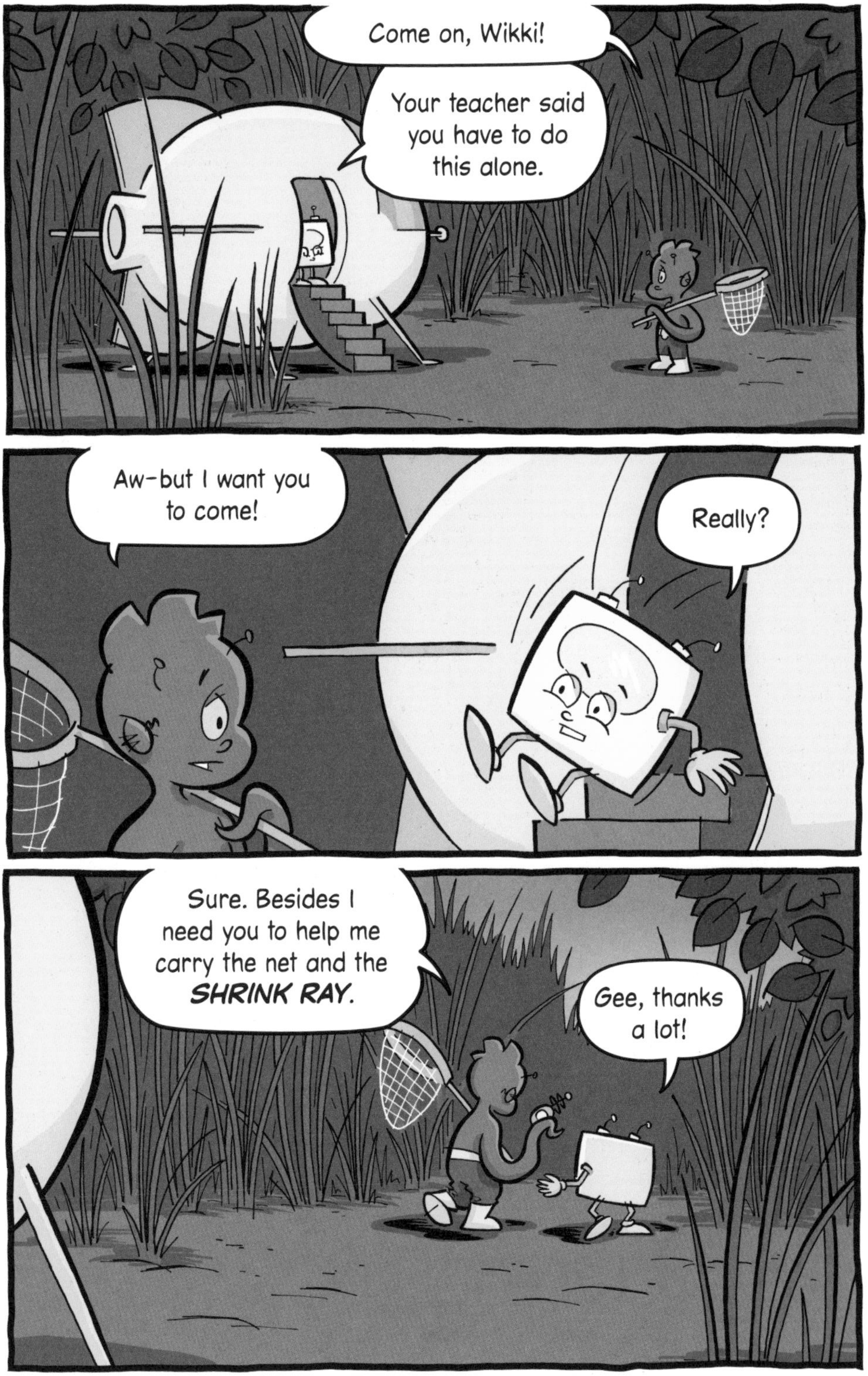
Come on, Wikki!
Your teacher said you have to do this alone.
Aw–but I want you to come!
Really?
Sure. Besides I need you to help me carry the net and the ***SHRINK RAY***.
Gee, thanks a lot!

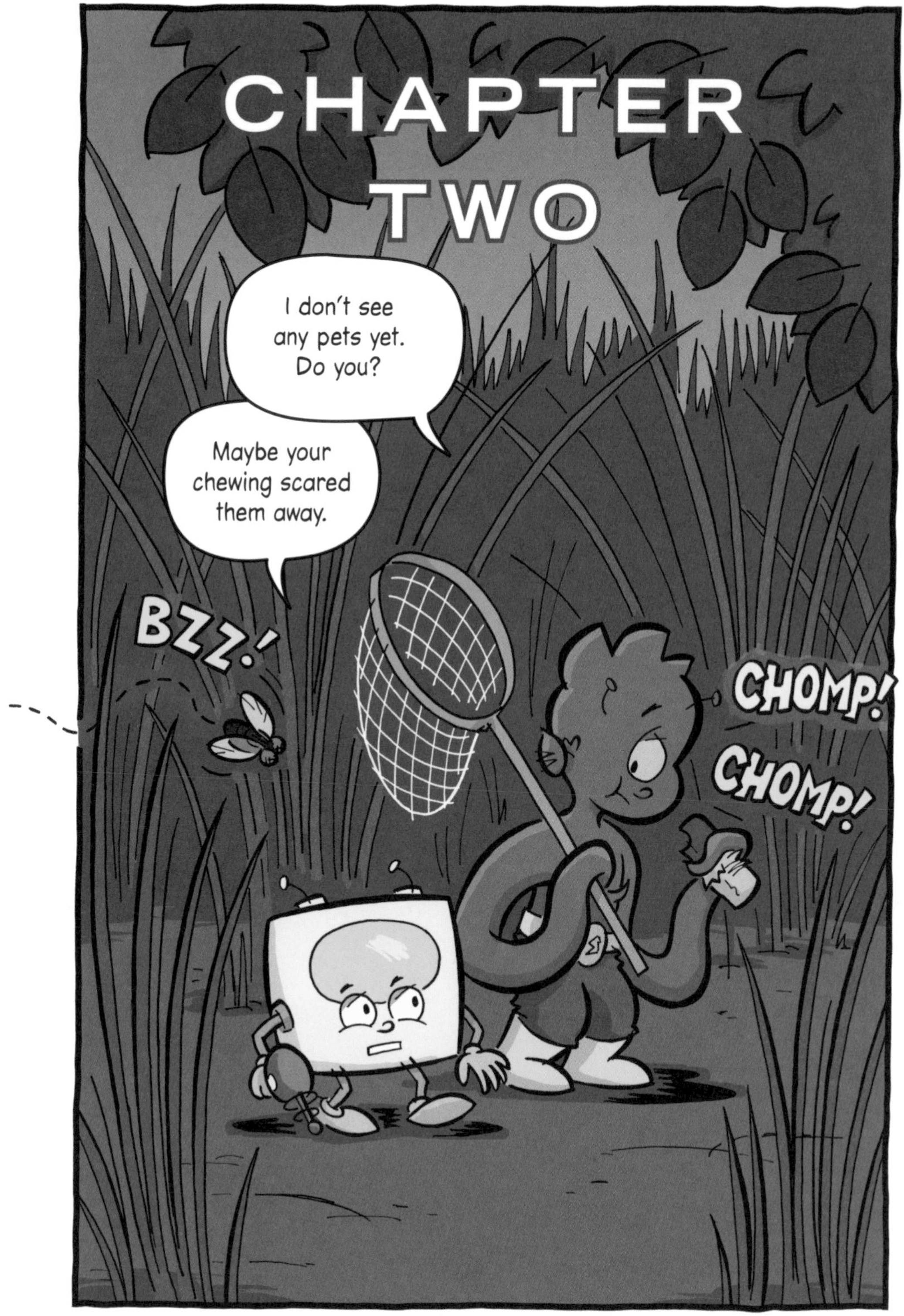
CHAPTER TWO
I don't see any pets yet. Do you?
Maybe your chewing scared them away.
BZZ!
CHOMP!
CHOMP!

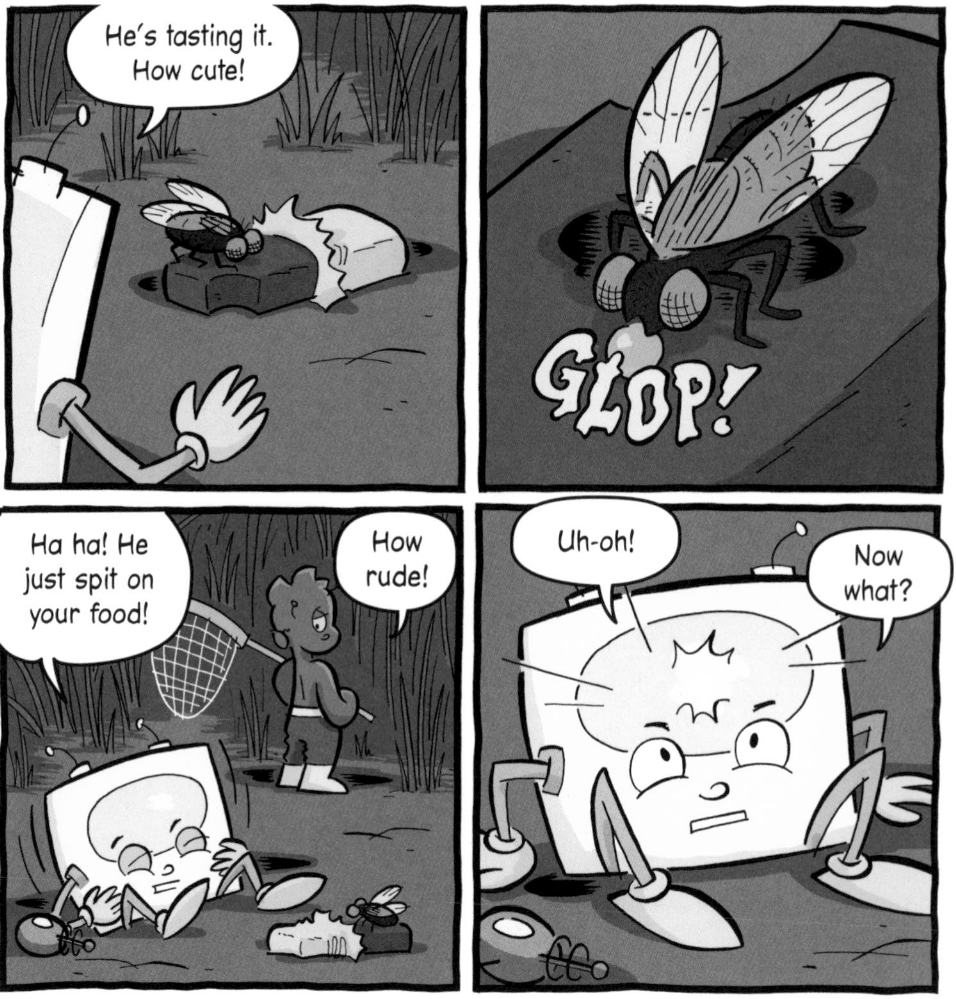
He's tasting it. How cute!
GLOP!
Ha ha! He just spit on your food!
How rude!
Uh-oh!
Now what?

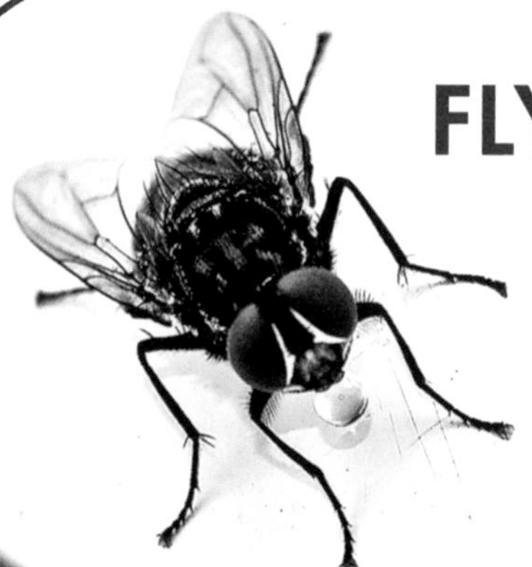

FLY spitting

FLIES USE SPIT TO TURN THEIR FOOD INTO LIQUID, THEN THEY SUCK IT UP AGAIN.

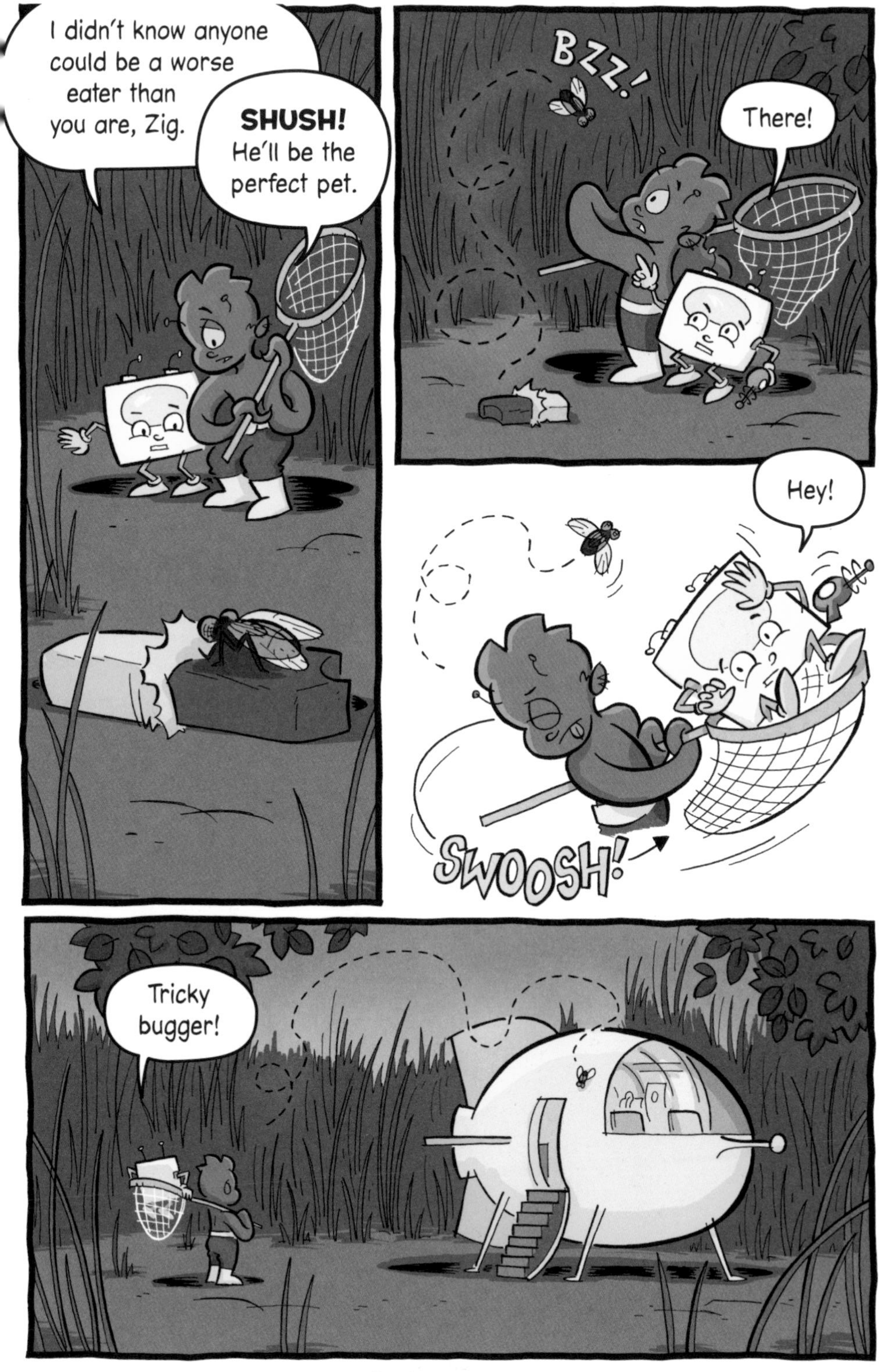
I didn't know anyone could be a worse eater than you are, Zig.
SHUSH! He'll be the perfect pet.
BZZ!
There!
Hey!
SWOOSH!
Tricky bugger!

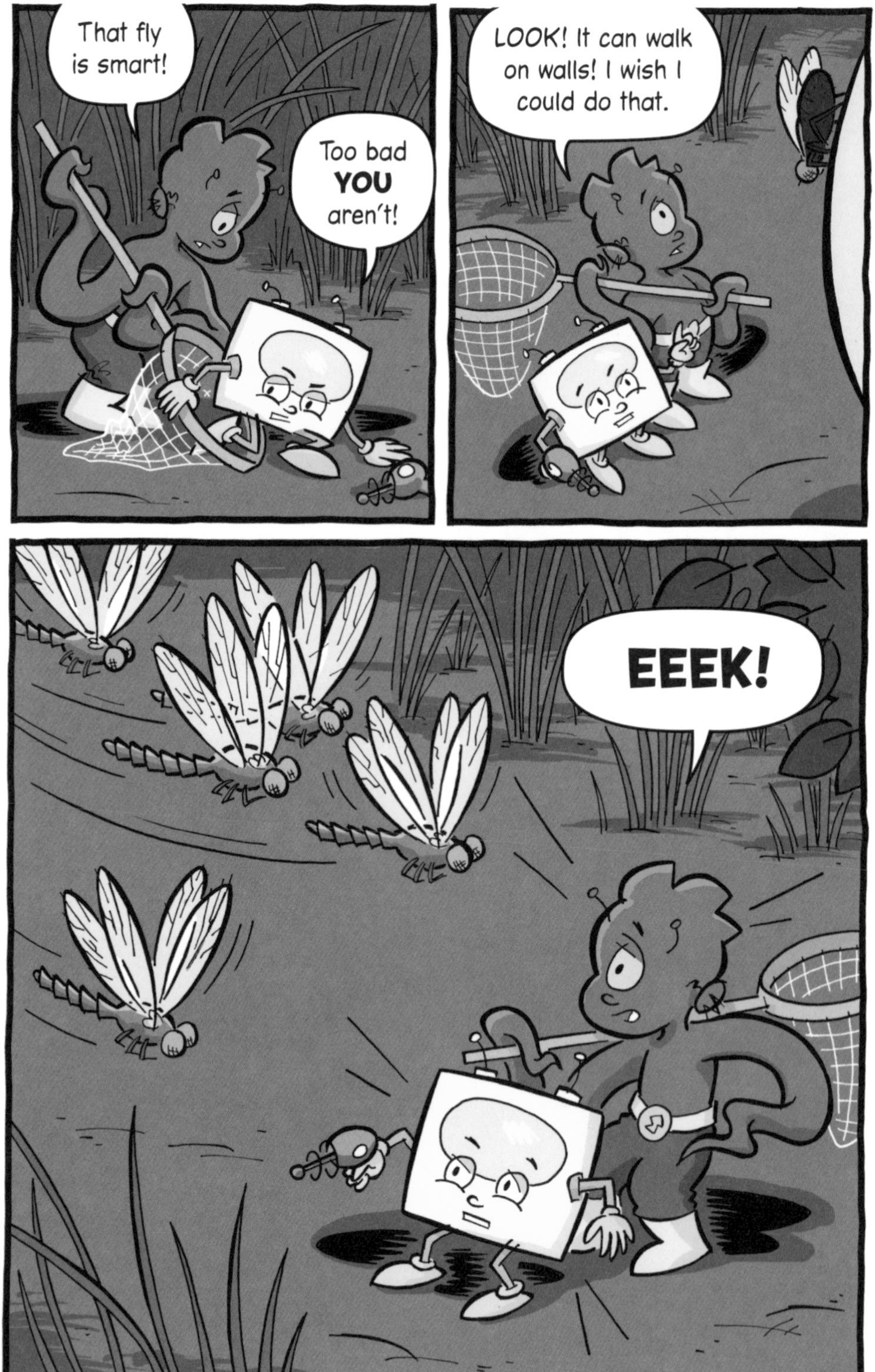
That fly is smart!
Too bad **YOU** aren't!
LOOK! It can walk on walls! I wish I could do that.
EEEK!

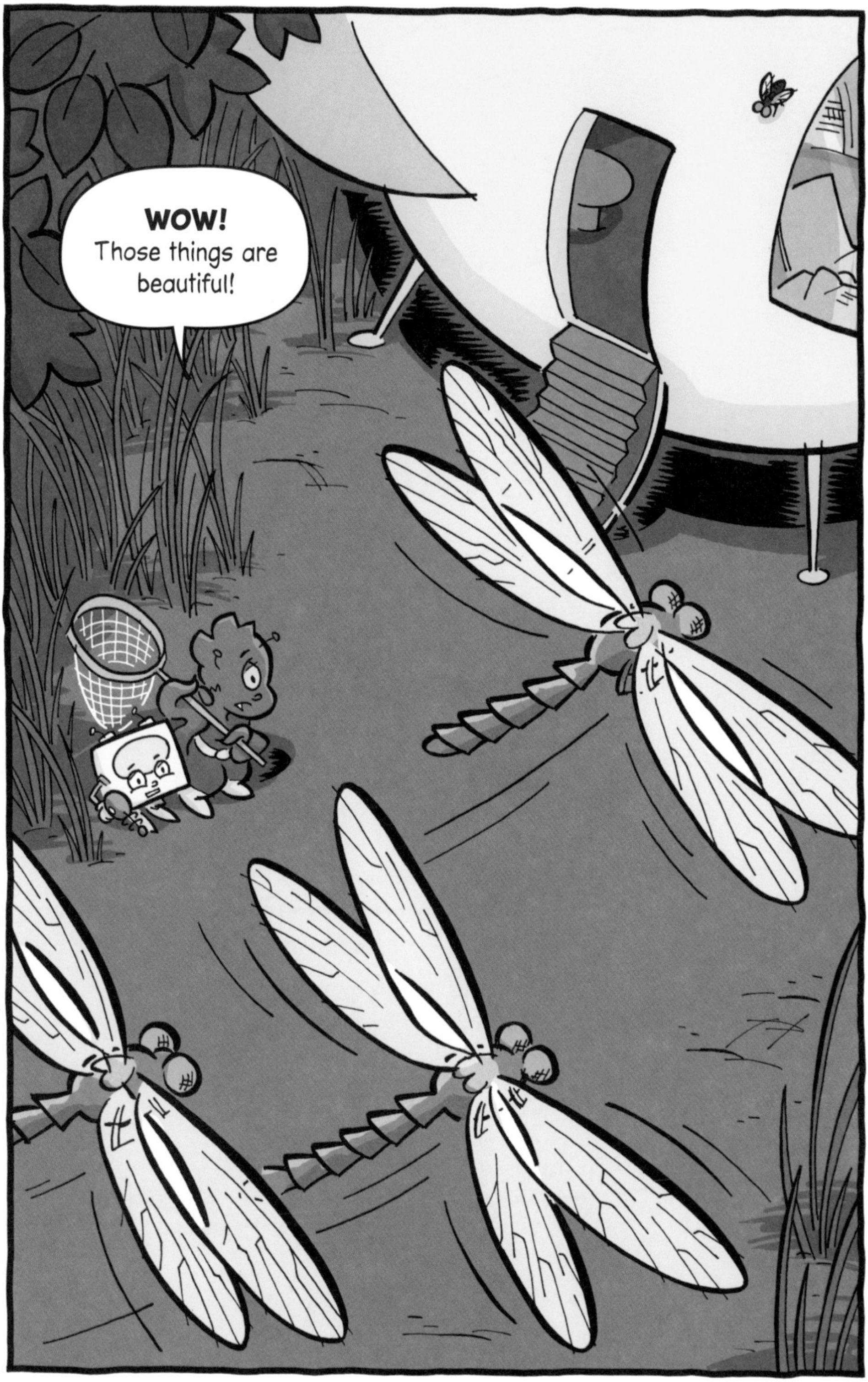
WOW!
Those things are beautiful!

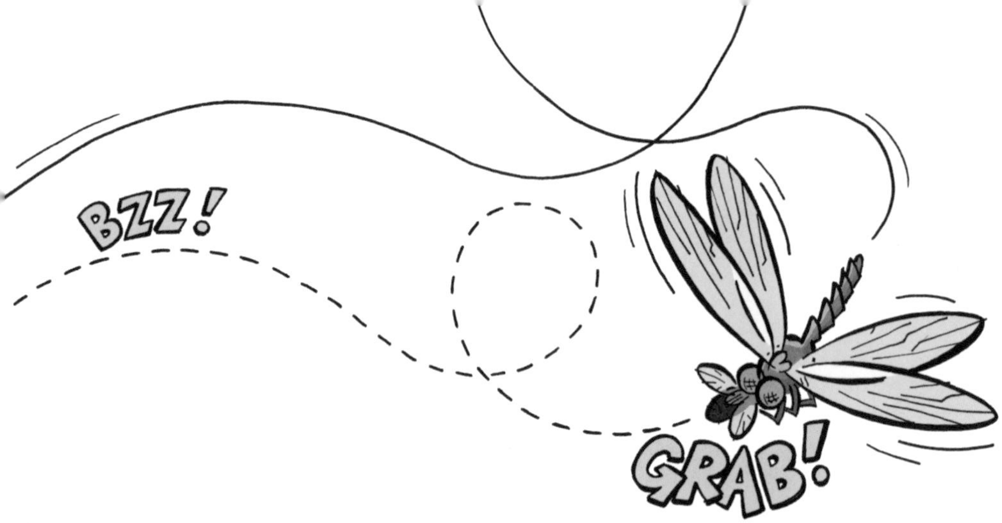
BZZ!
GRAB!

DRAGONFLY

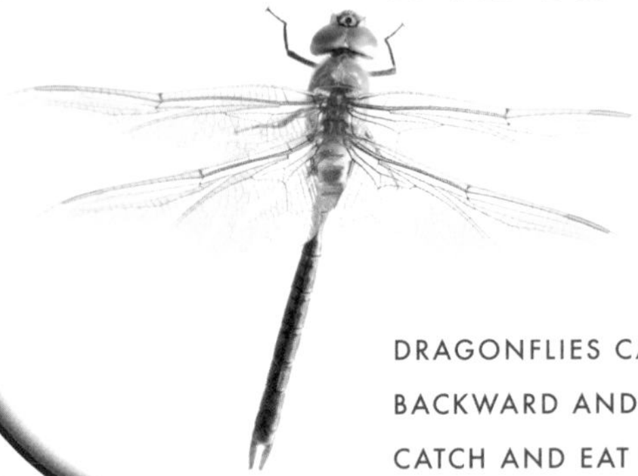

DRAGONFLIES CAN FLY FORWARD, BACKWARD AND SIDEWAYS. THEY CAN CATCH AND EAT PREY AS THEY FLY.

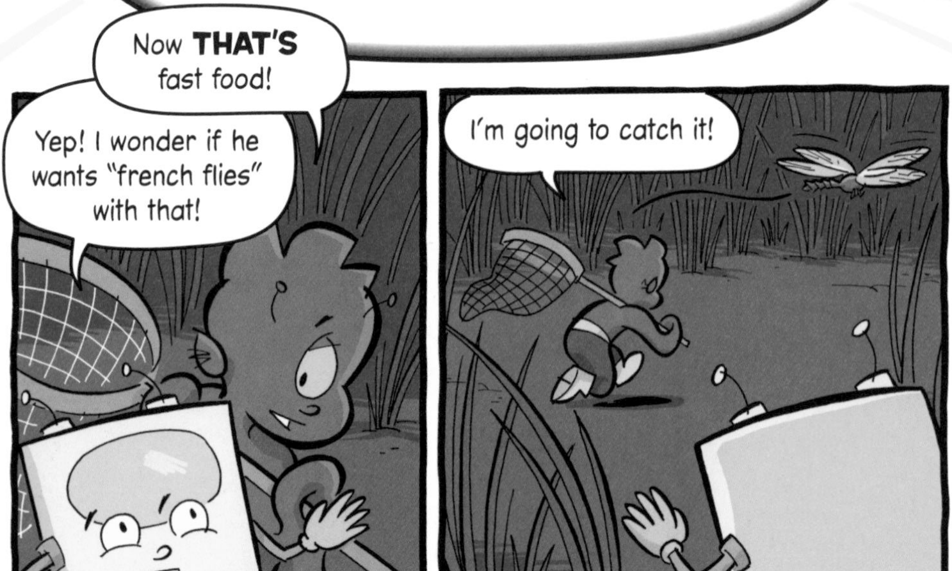
Now **THAT'S** fast food!
Yep! I wonder if he wants "french flies" with that!
I'm going to catch it!

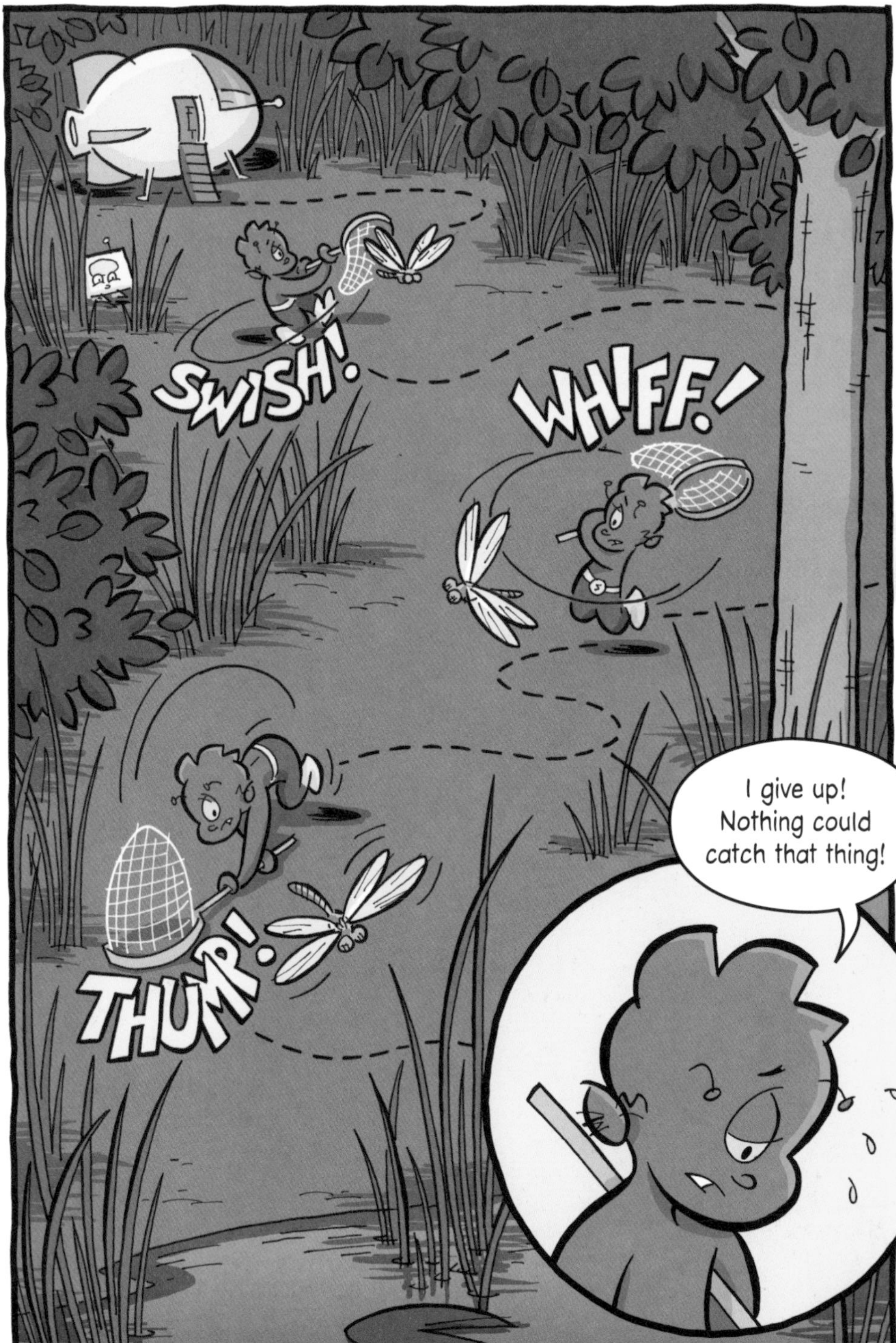
SWISH!
WHIFF!
THUMP!
I give up! Nothing could catch that thing!

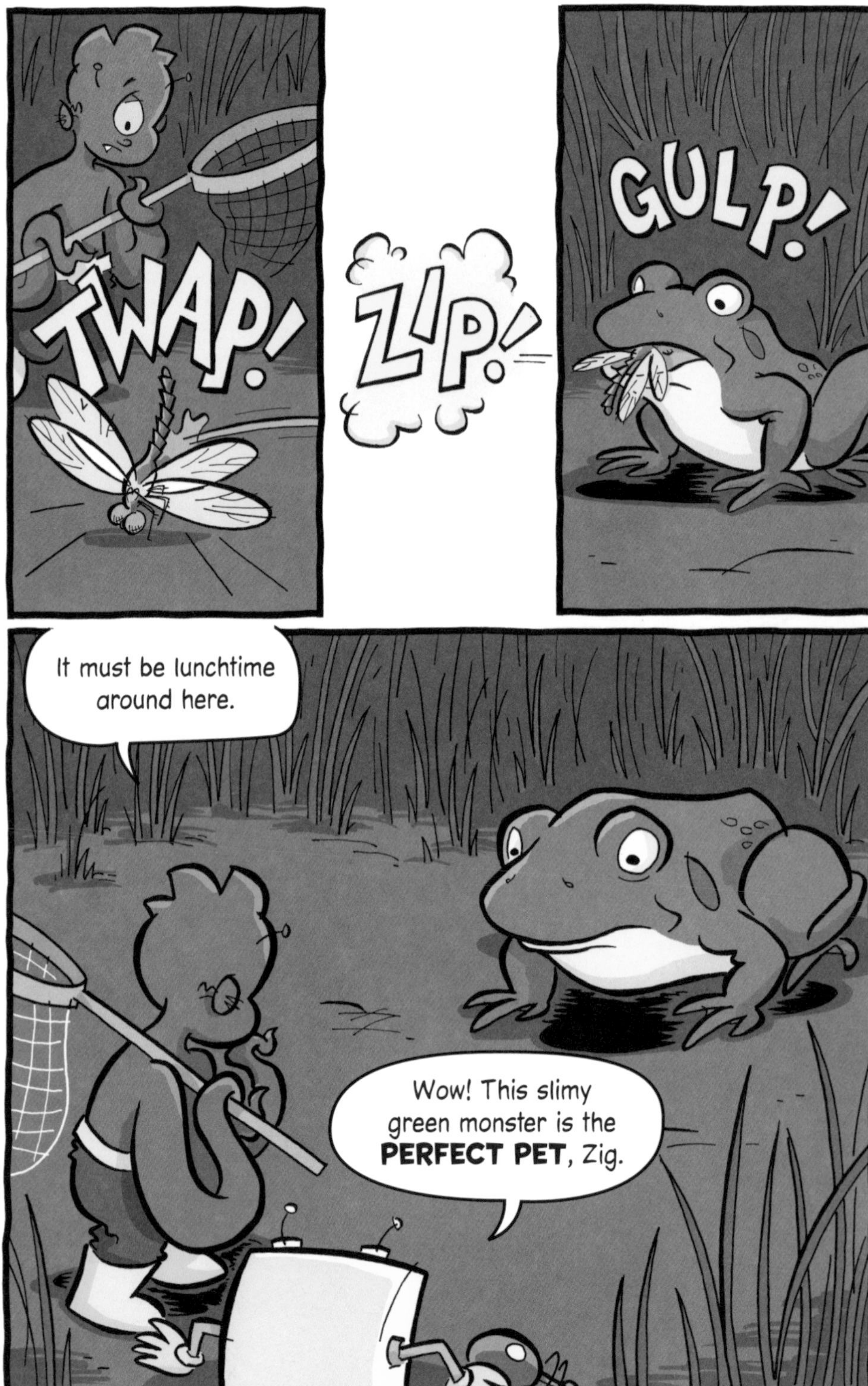
TWAP!
ZIP!
GULP!
It must be lunchtime around here.
Wow! This slimy green monster is the PERFECT PET, Zig.

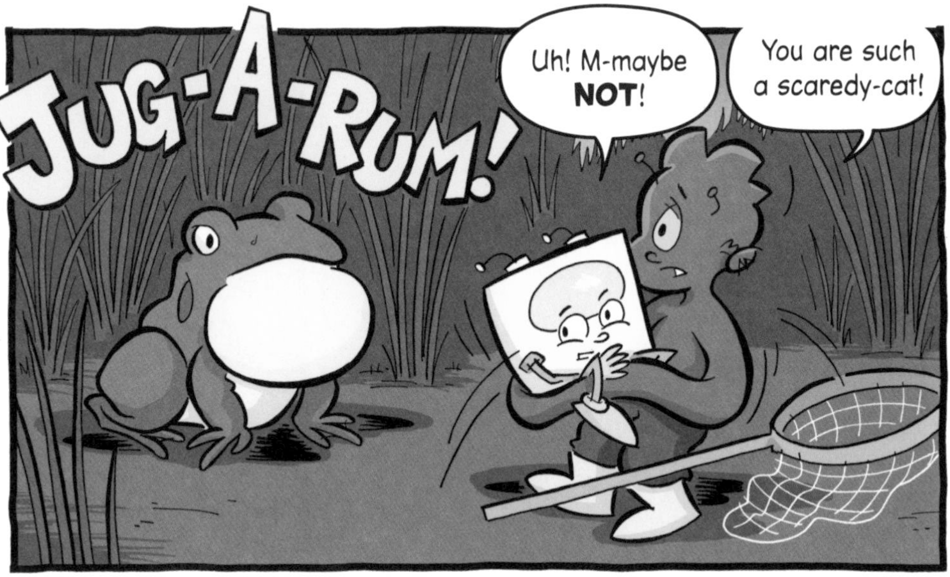
JUG-A-RUM!
Uh! M-maybe **NOT**!
You are such a scaredy-cat!

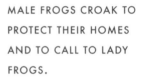

FROG croaking

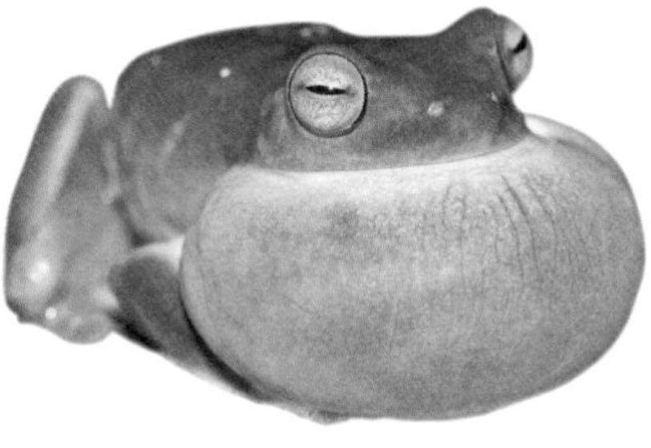

MALE FROGS CROAK TO PROTECT THEIR HOMES AND TO CALL TO LADY FROGS.

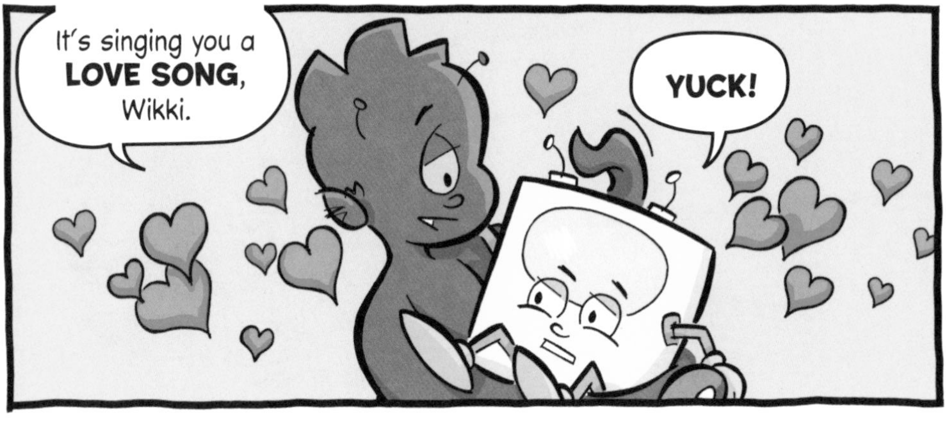
It's singing you a **LOVE SONG**, Wikki.
YUCK!

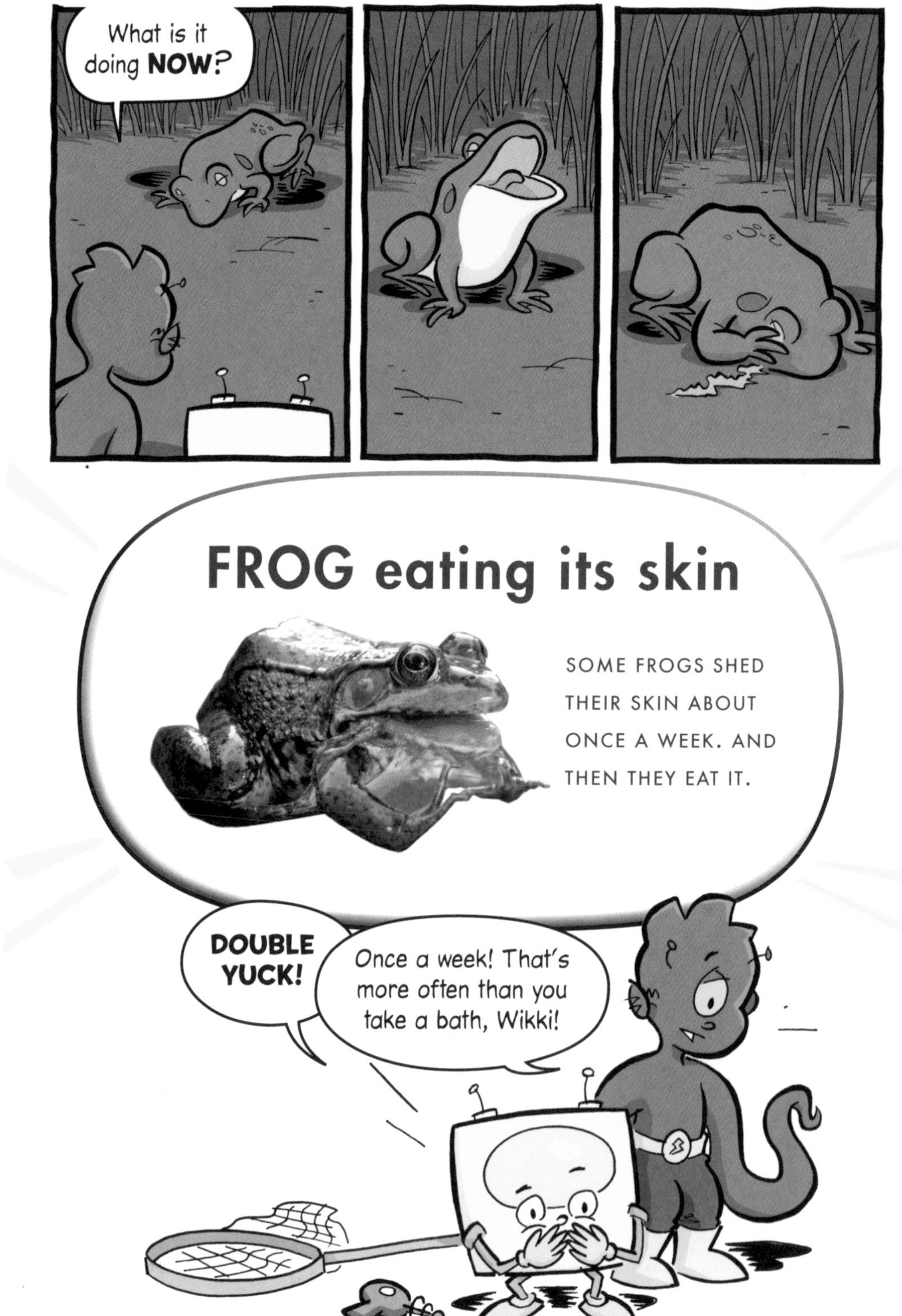
What is it doing **NOW?**
FROG eating its skin
SOME FROGS SHED THEIR SKIN ABOUT ONCE A WEEK. AND THEN THEY EAT IT.
DOUBLE YUCK!
Once a week! That's more often than you take a bath, Wikki!

23

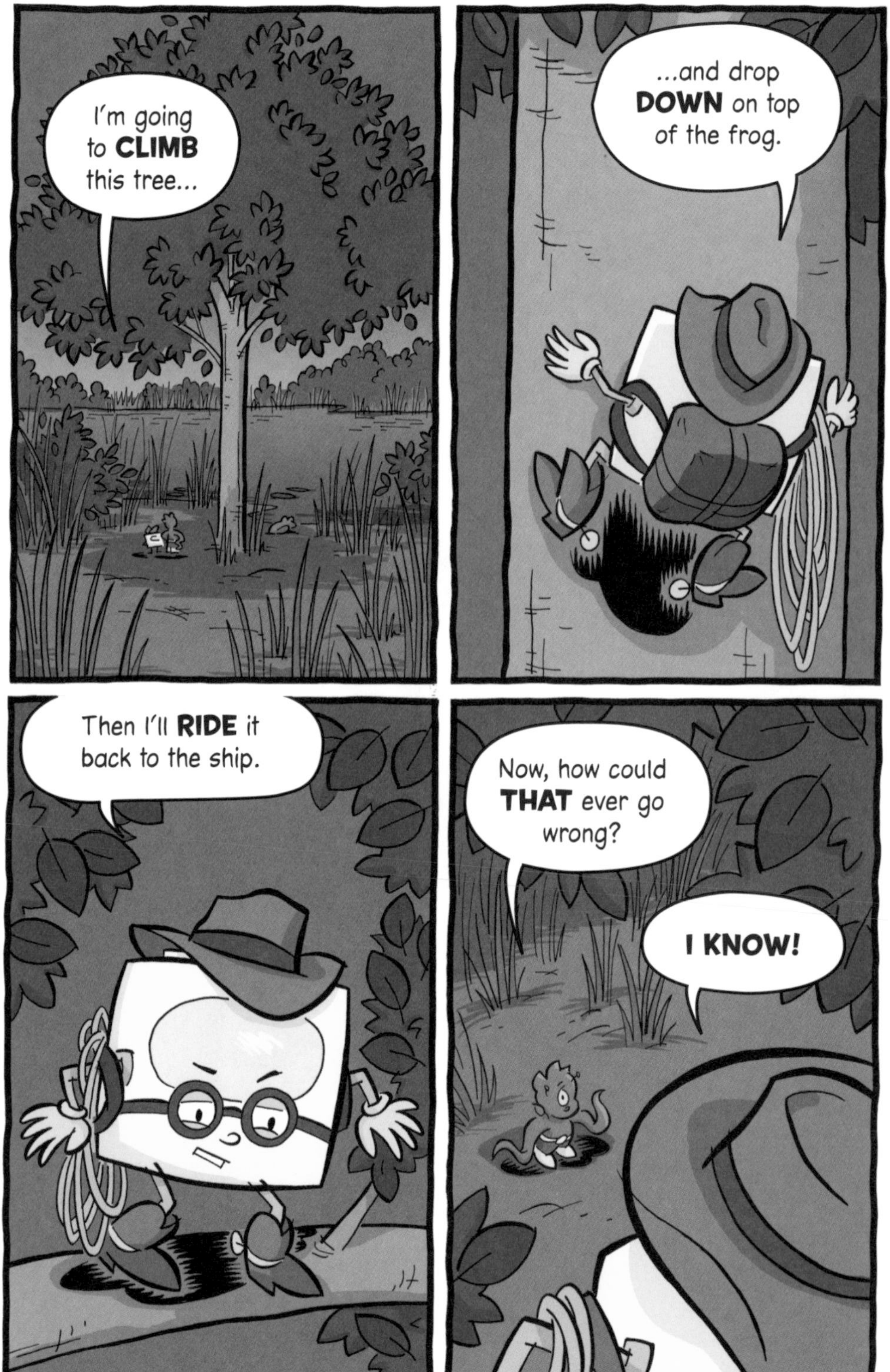
I'm going to **CLIMB** this tree...
...and drop **DOWN** on top of the frog.
Then I'll **RIDE** it back to the ship.
Now, how could **THAT** ever go wrong?
I KNOW!

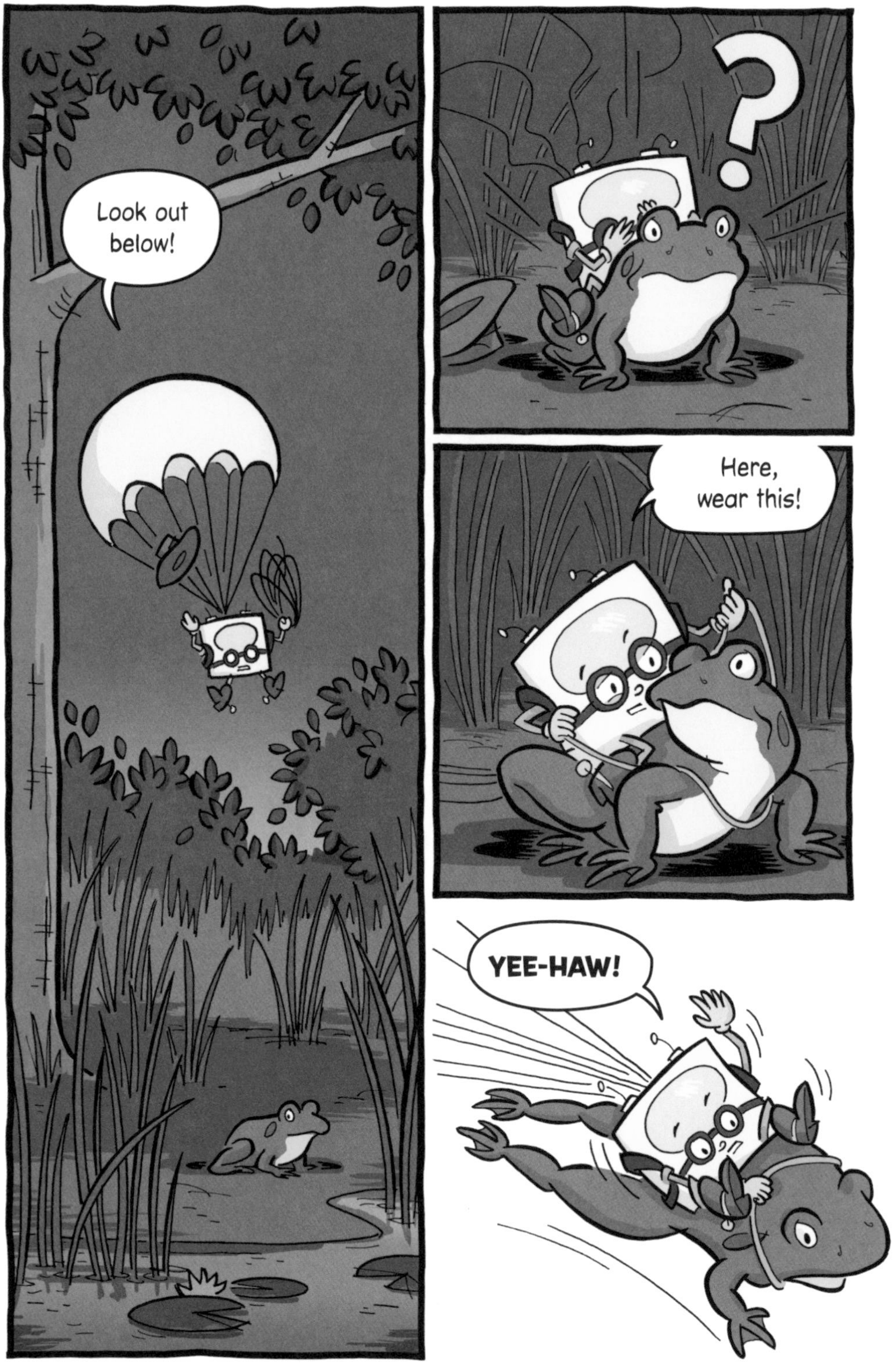
Look out below!
?
Here, wear this!
YEE-HAW!

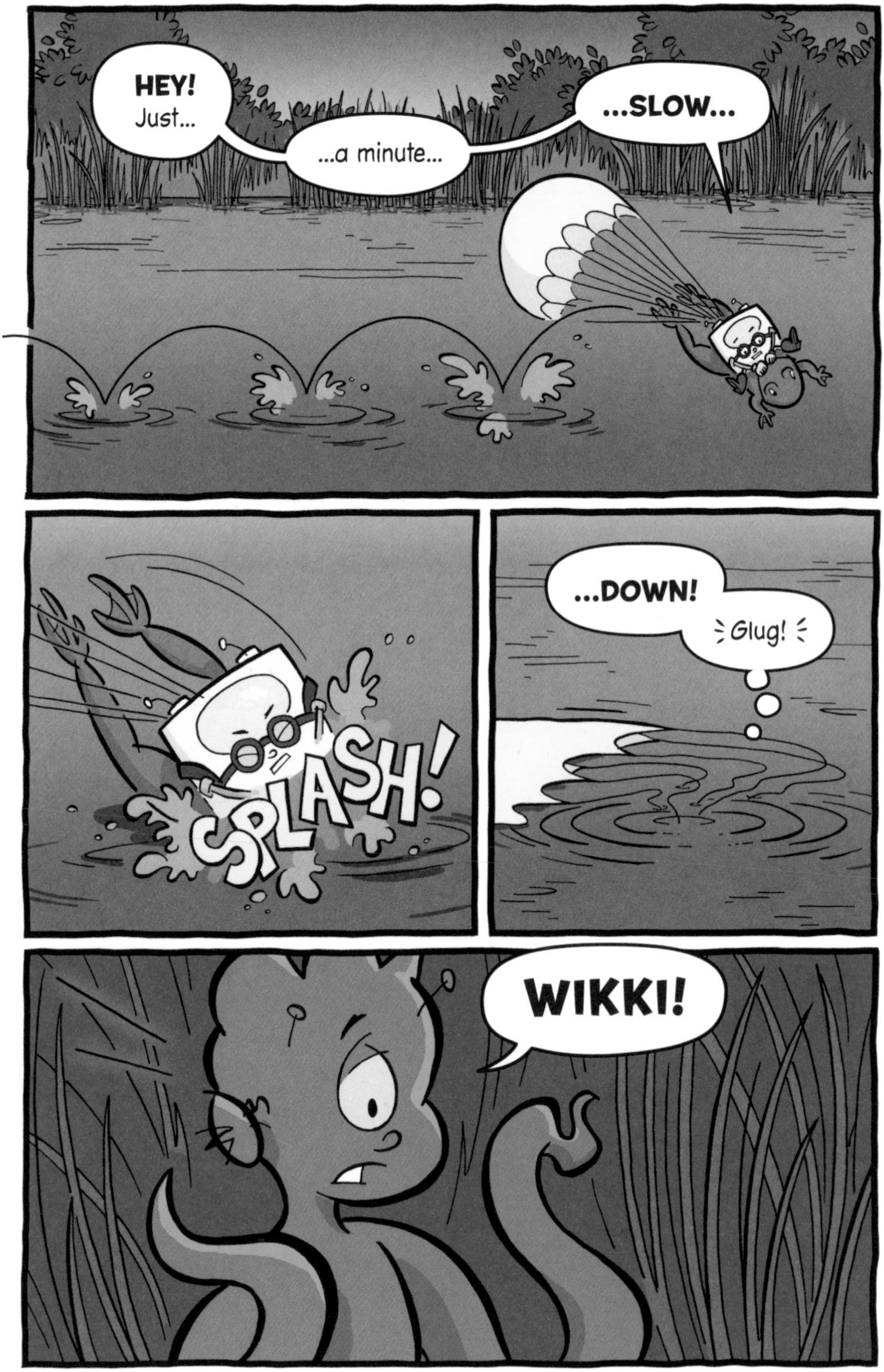
HEY!
Just...
...a minute...
...SLOW...
SPLASH!
...DOWN!
Glug!
WIKKI!

27

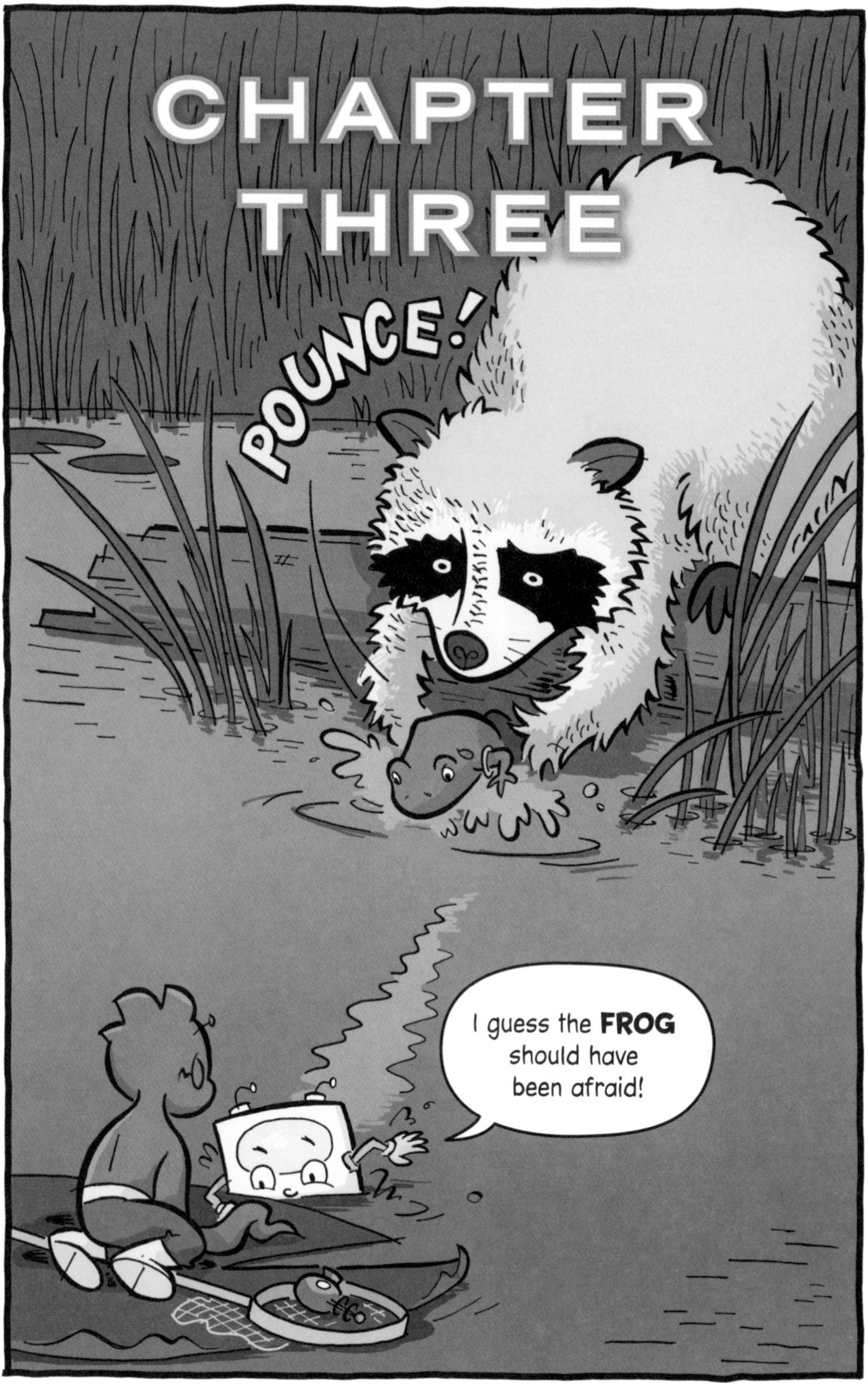
CHAPTER THREE
POUNCE!
I guess the **FROG** should have been afraid!

RACCOON hand

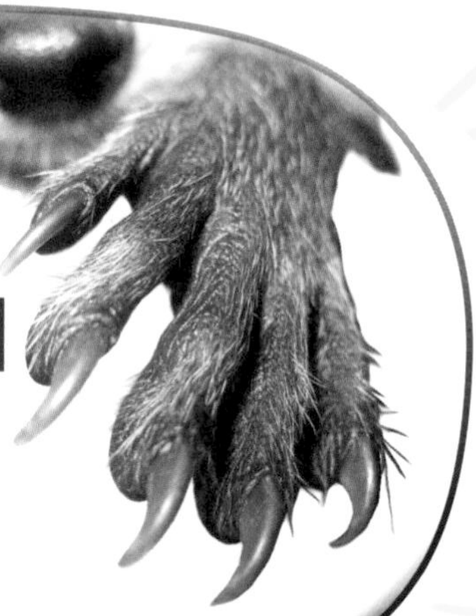

RACCOONS HAVE FIVE FINGERS ON EACH HAND, WHICH COME IN HANDY!

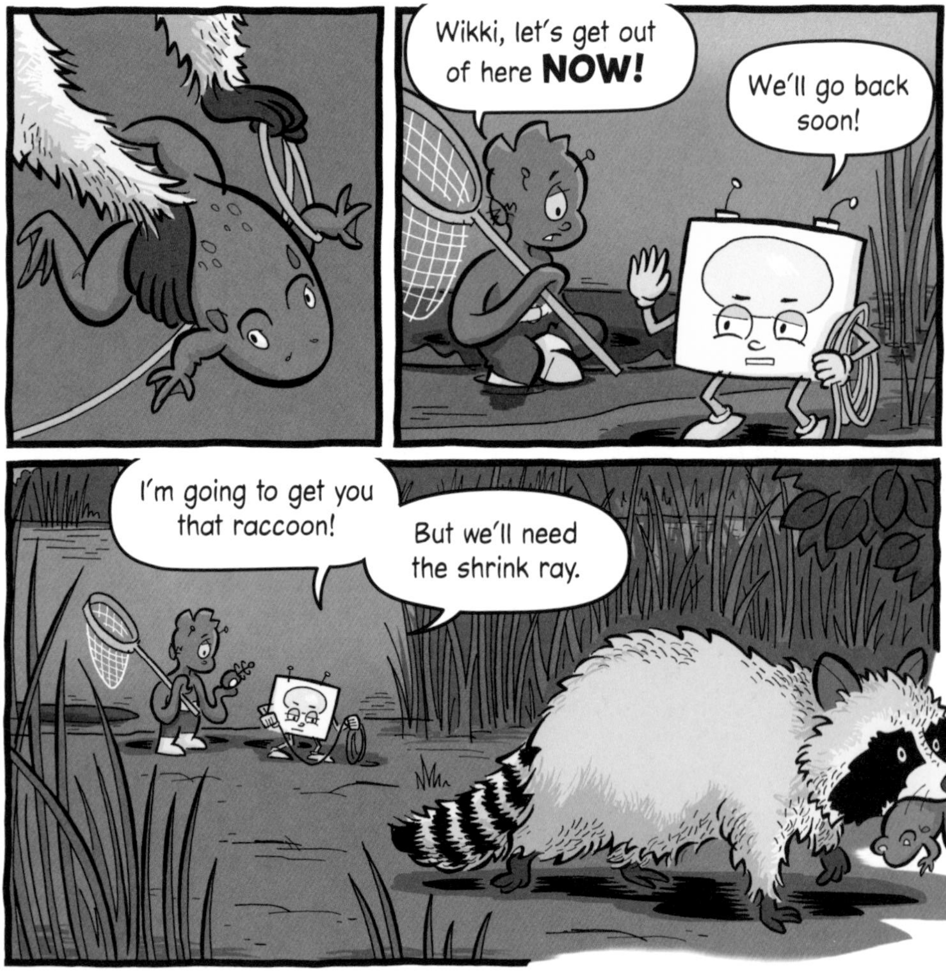
Wikki, let's get out of here **NOW!**
We'll go back soon!
I'm going to get you that raccoon!
But we'll need the shrink ray.

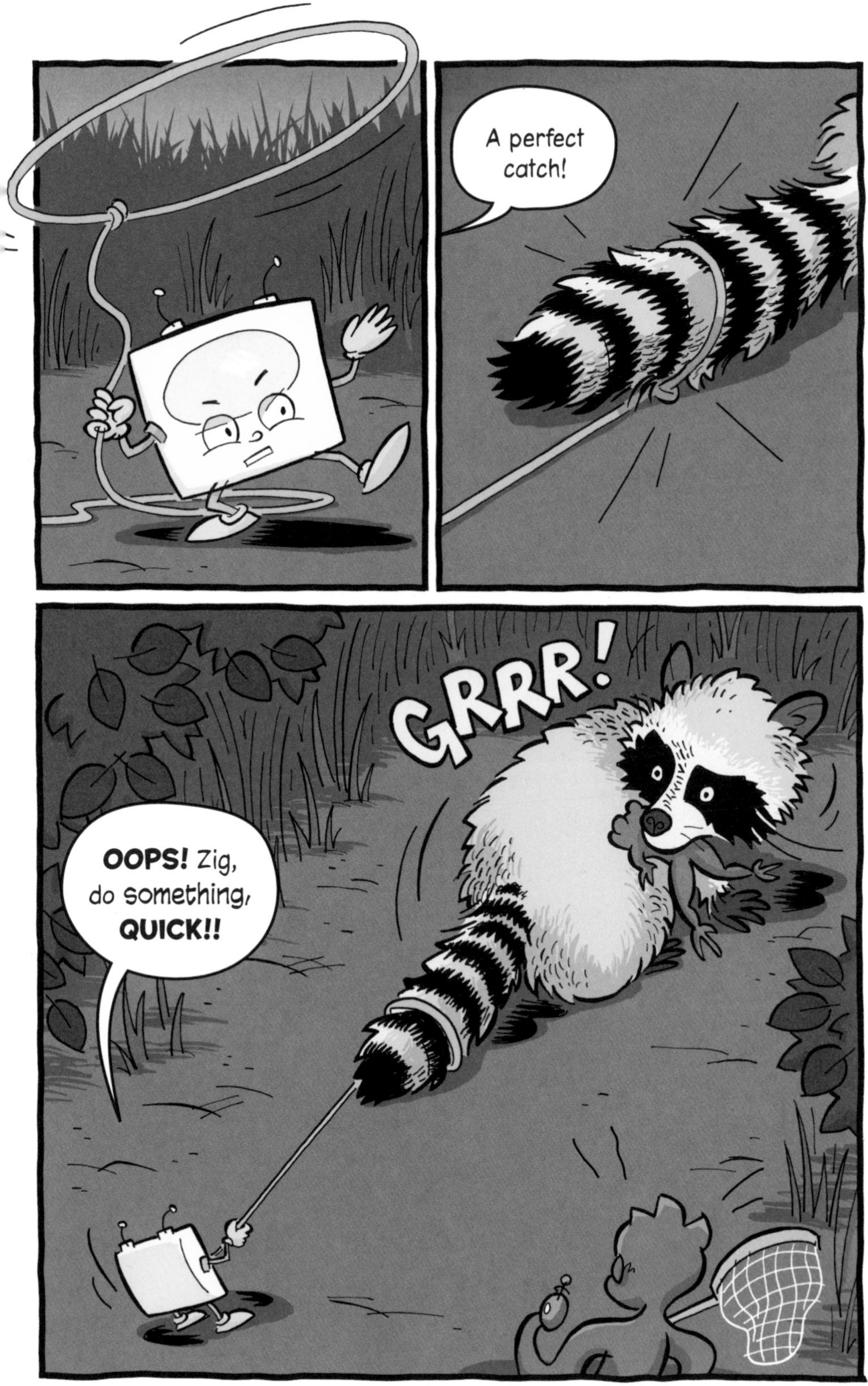
A perfect catch!
GRRR!
OOPS! Zig, do something, QUICK!!

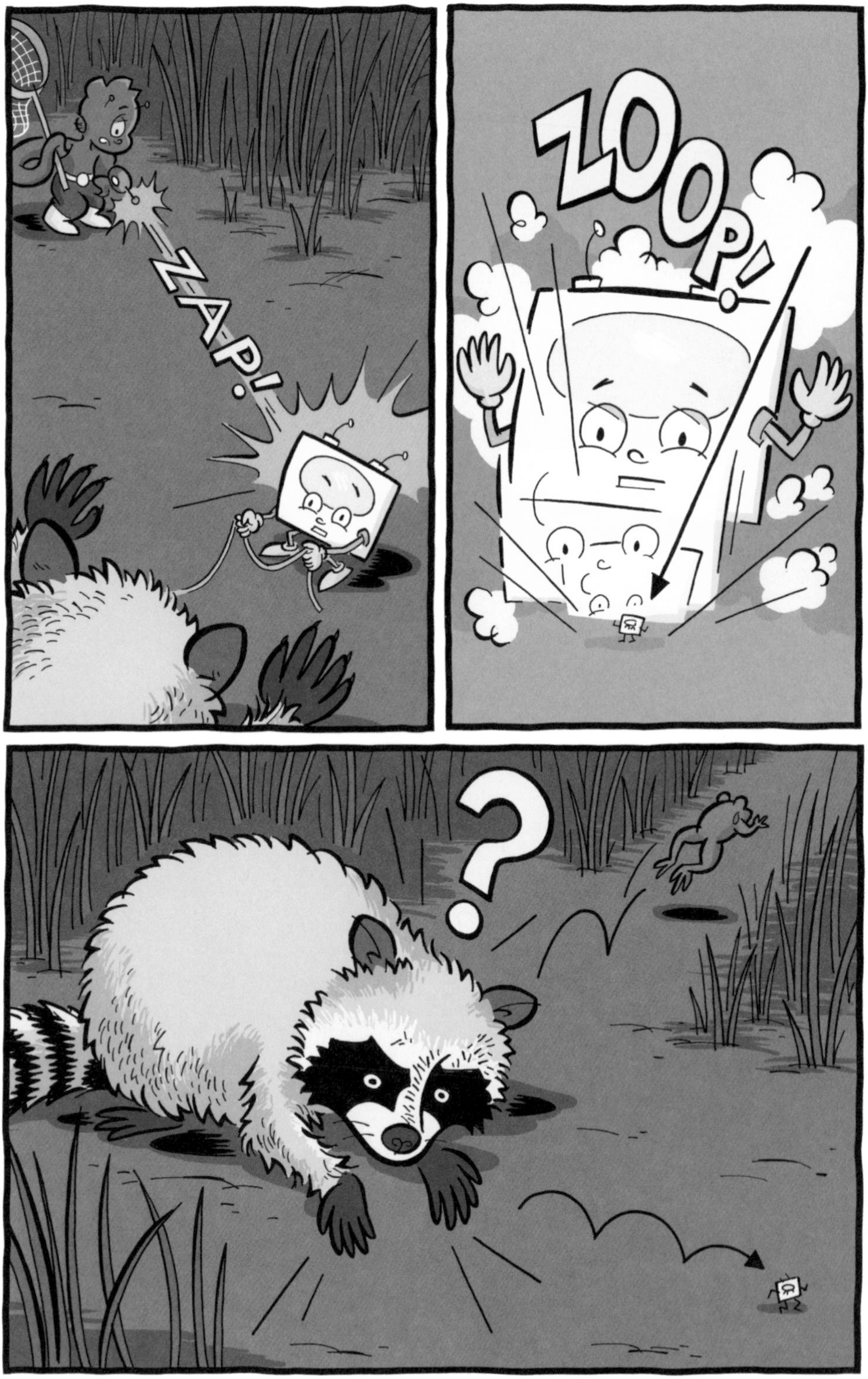
ZAP!
ZOOP!
?

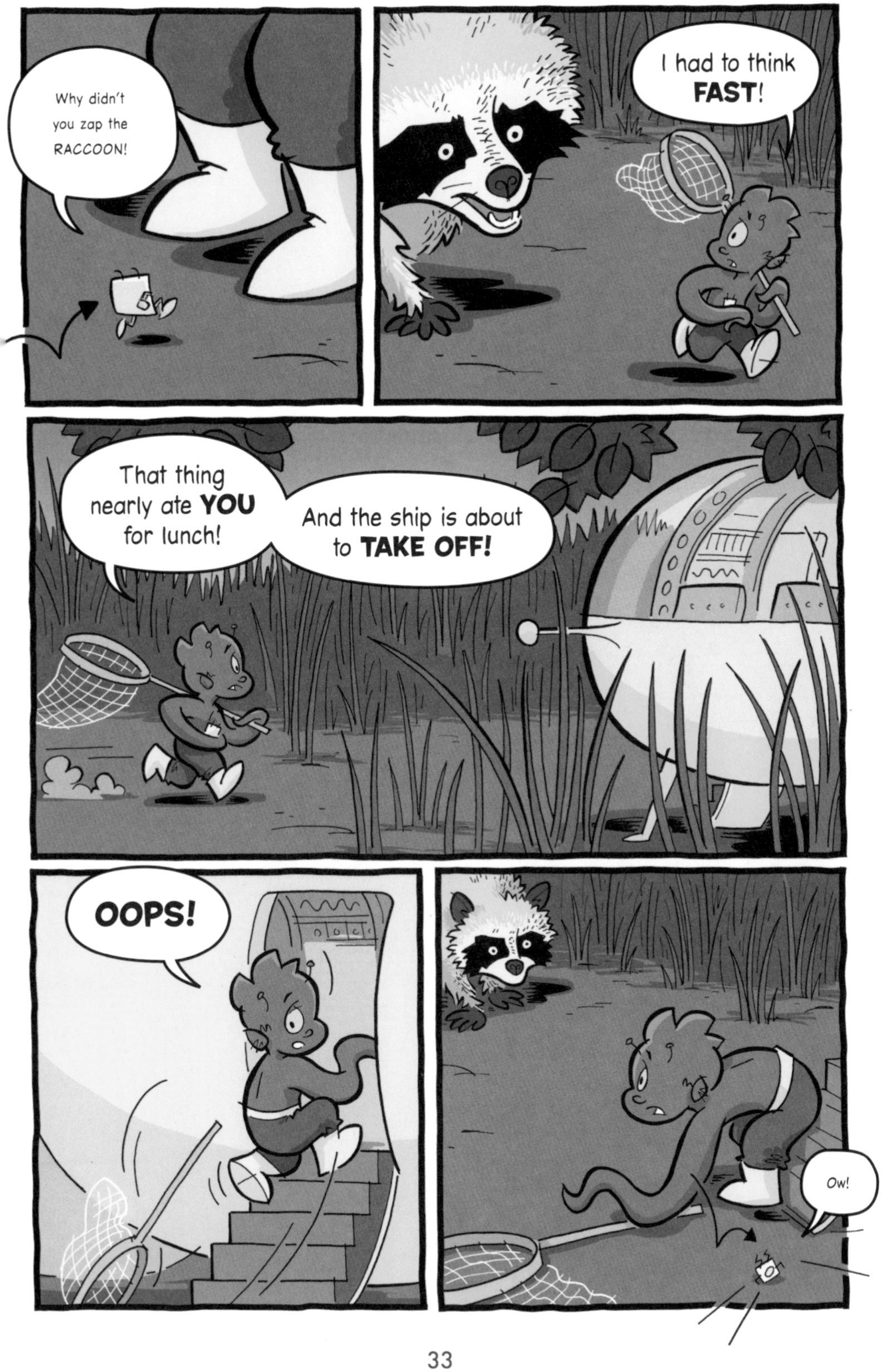
Why didn't you zap the RACCOON!
I had to think FAST!
That thing nearly ate YOU for lunch!
And the ship is about to TAKE OFF!
OOPS!
Ow!

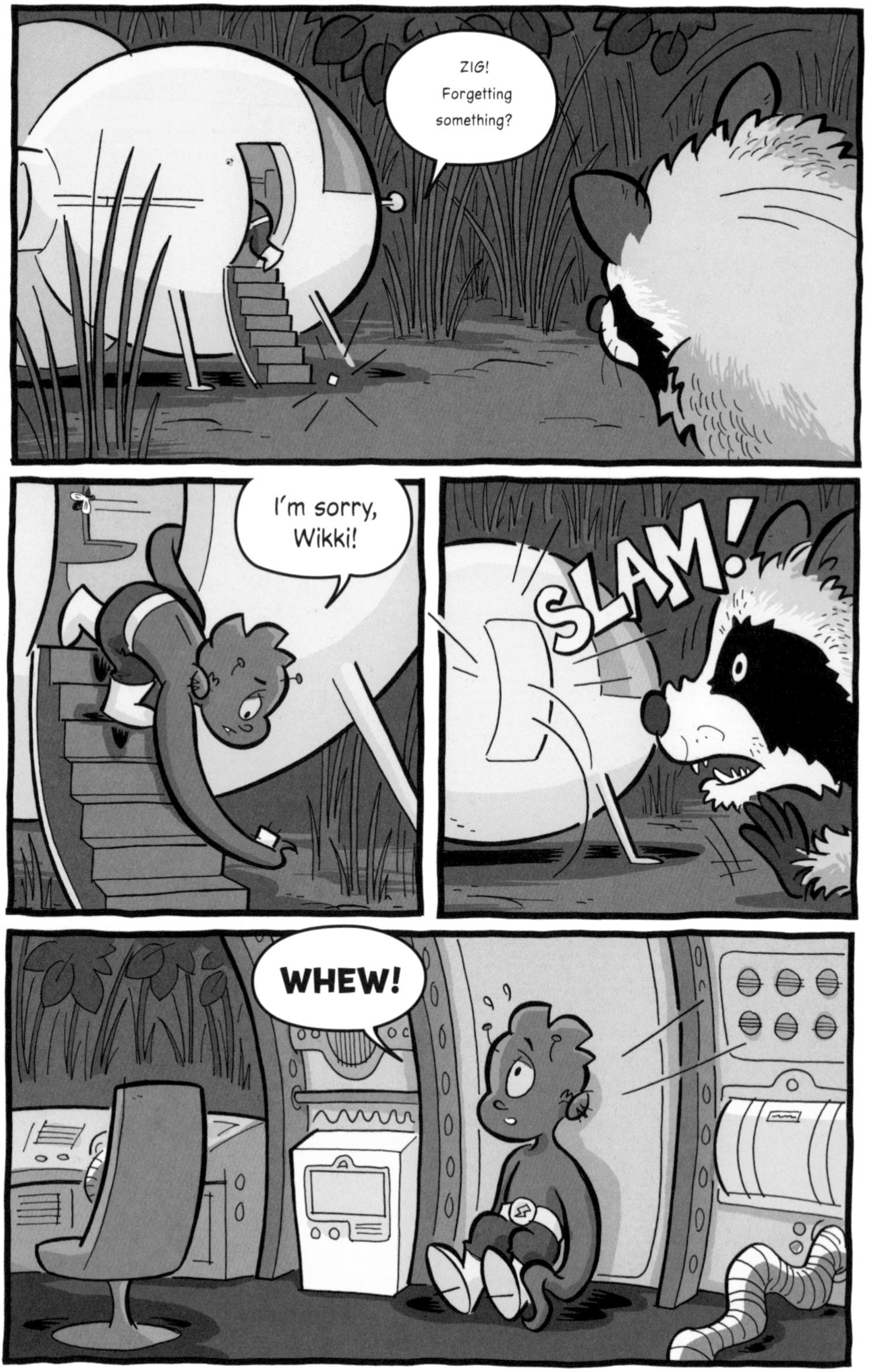
ZIG! Forgetting something?
I'm sorry, Wikki!
SLAM!
WHEW!

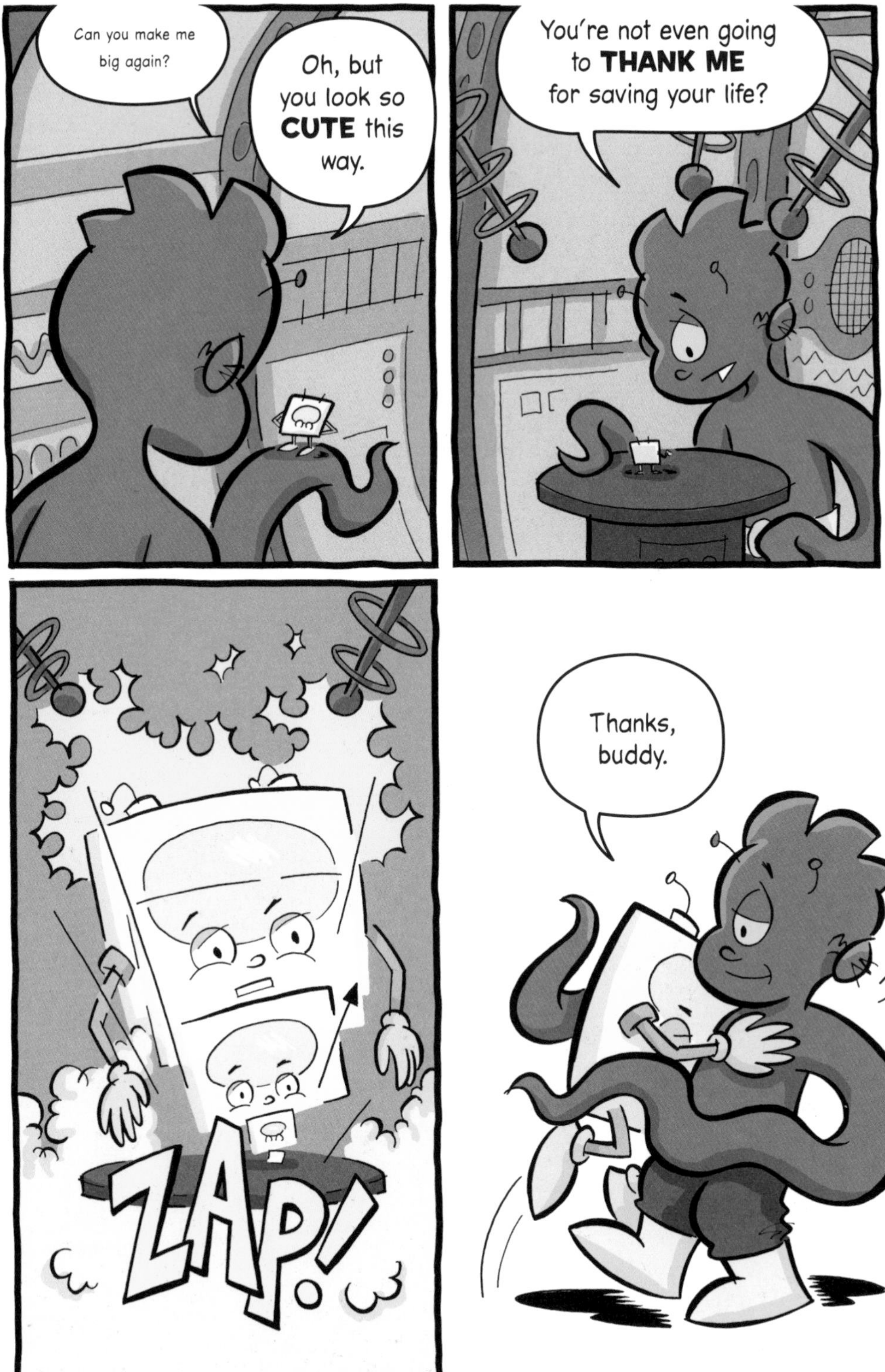
Can you make me big again?
Oh, but you look so **CUTE** this way.
You're not even going to **THANK ME** for saving your life?
ZAP!
Thanks, buddy.

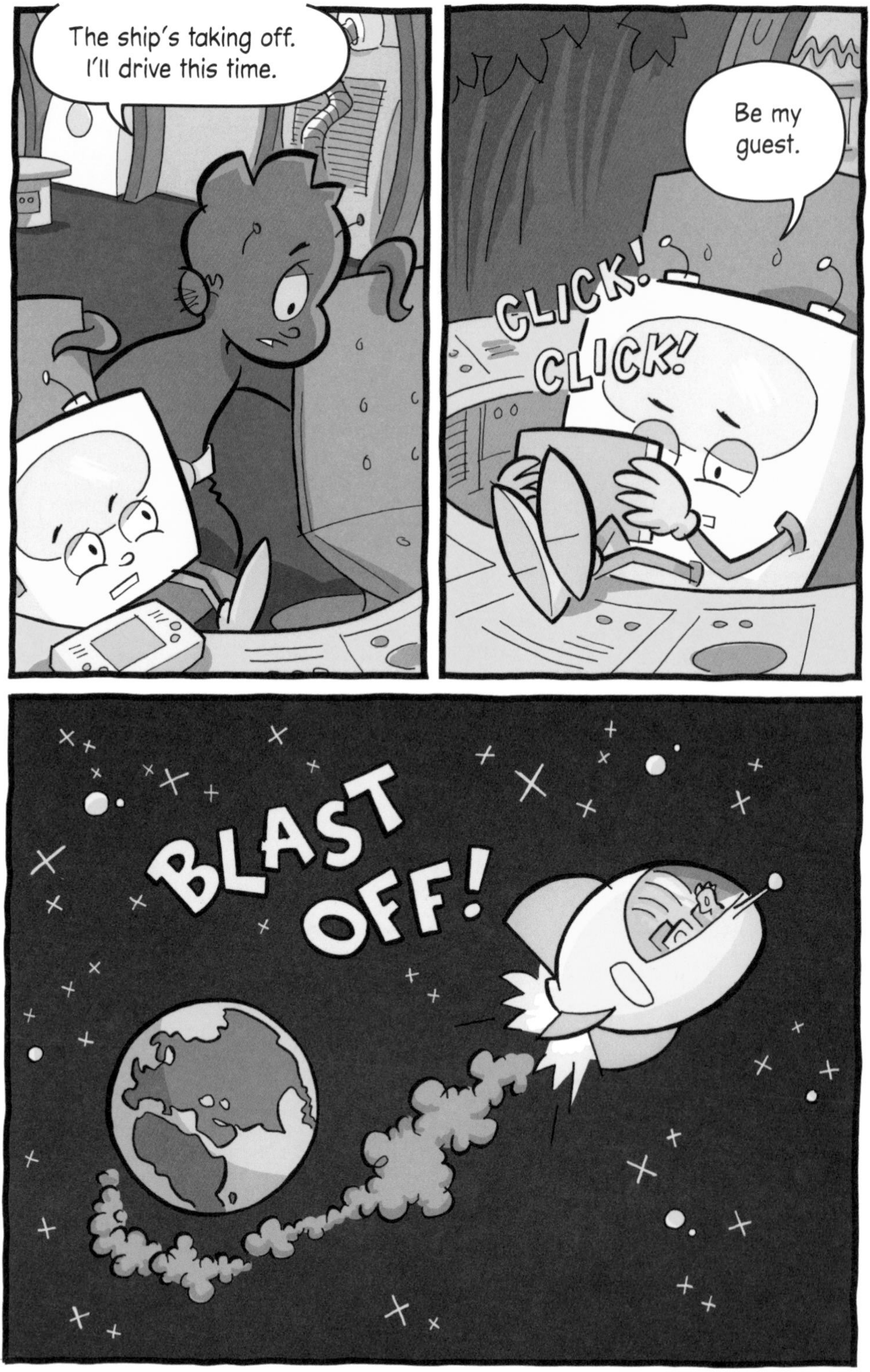
The ship's taking off. I'll drive this time.
Be my guest.
CLICK!
CLICK!
BLAST OFF!

37

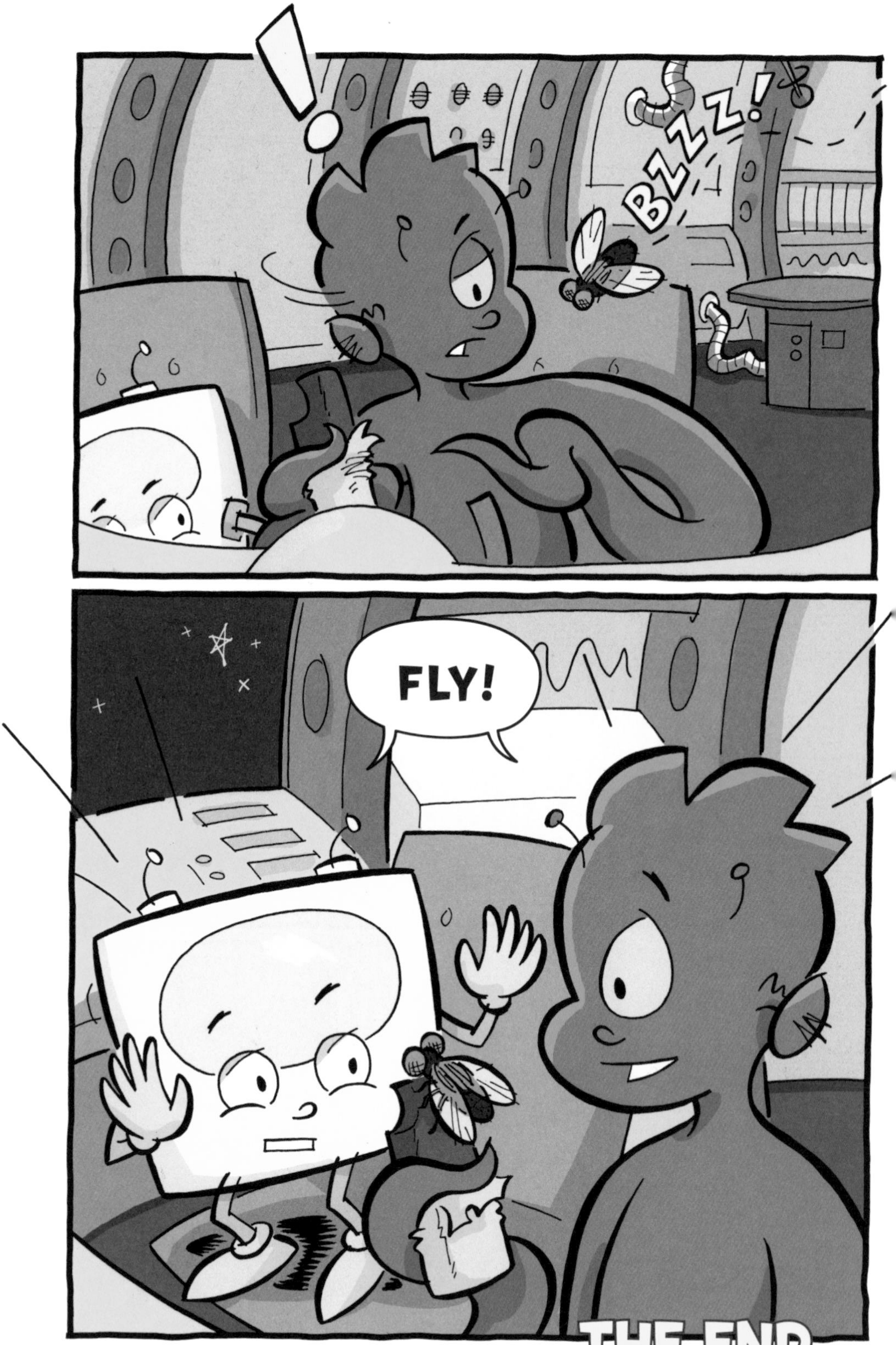
!
BZZZ!
FLY!
THE END

ABOUT THE AUTHORS

NADJA SPIEGELMAN, who wrote Zig and Wikki's story, recently graduated from Yale University as an English major. She grew up in New York City where there are few dragonflies and frogs, although there are certainly plenty of houseflies. When she was younger, she loved going to the country, where she collected insects and salamanders and kept them inside her shoe-box "bug museum." This is her first book.

TRADE LOEFFLER, who drew Zig and Wikki, grew up in Livermore, California. Unlike Zig and Wikki, he doesn't believe flies make good pets. But he did like to collect them when he was a kid—to feed them to the funnel spiders that lived in a field near his house. Trade now lives in New York City with his wife, Annalisa; son, Clark; and dog, Boo. He is the creator of the all-ages web comic *Zip and Li'l Bit* but this TOON book is Trade's first-ever work in print.

WIKKI'S FUN FACTS

FLIES START OUT AS SMALL WORMLIKE LARVAE, THEN MAKE COCOONS IN WHICH THEY BECOME ADULT FLIES.

DRAGONFLIES CAN EACH EAT UP TO **300** MOSQUITOES A DAY.

FROGS HAVE EYES THAT STICK OUT TO GIVE THEM PANORAMIC (ALL-AROUND) VISION. THEY SQUEEZE THEIR EYEBALLS IN TO HELP SWALLOW.

RACCOONS STORE THE EXTRA FAT THEY NEED FOR THE WINTER IN THEIR TAILS.

Come visit us at...
TOON-BOOKS
.com

TOON READERS: a free, revolutionary online tool that allows all readers to *TOON INTO READING!*

Come listen to the authors read their books aloud while you click on the balloons and turn the pages. The TOON READERS are also offered in Spanish, French, Russian, Chinese, and other languages, a breakthrough for all readers including English Language Learners.

Young READERS can be young WRITERS: make your own cartoon with Zig and Wikki, or with other TOON characters. Use our free CARTOON MAKER and send us your cartoon; we'll post the best ones online for everyone to read.

Come read your friends' cartoons and check TOON-BOOKS.com regularly for videos, games, contests, and more!